DEAD IN THE WATER

TOM TURNER

SERENA TURNER

TRIBECA PRESS

JOIN TOM'S AUTHOR NEWSLETTER

Get the latest news on Tom's upcoming novels when you sign up for his free author newsletter at **tomturnerbooks.com/news**.

ONE

THE MAN TOOK a ferocious cut at the golf ball, like he wanted to drive it all the way to dry land ten miles away. The ball sliced out over the dark grey ocean, skipped twice and splashed. He teed up another one.

A man on the deck below dove into the infinity-edge pool. The dive came painfully close to a belly flop. Give him a three out of ten.

Below him, a third man shouted "pull" and a clay pigeon was launched out over the water. The man squeezed the trigger of his elegant shotgun and the clay pigeon shattered like Fourth of July fireworks.

On the main deck, a fourth man was knocking back his second Bloody Mary of the day, chatting up the cute bartender, who doubled as a croupier at the craps table at night.

All five of them were on board the seventh largest yacht in the world, the spectacular 430-foot-long *Miss Adventure,* which was presently ten miles off the coast of Palm Beach, Florida. The golfer was hitting balls from a tee on a round deck suspended out over the ocean like a shimmering white frisbee. The man in the infinity edge pool had boasted to his friends that he was going to do twenty laps, but petered out after two and a half. The man with the shotgun was on a platform cantilevered above the starboard rail, and the one with tomato juice, tabasco sauce and vodka in his neatly clipped mustache was watching a large helicopter float down toward a helipad. It resembled Marine One, the presidential chopper, but was painted a striking teal green.

On the aft deck was perched the yacht's tender—a gleaming red Ferrari. The *Miss Adventure,* regarded as one of the most magnificent, aerodynamic designs on the ocean today, was sleek, streamlined and shark-like. With six decks, its signature feature was a round, glass-walled, double-story salon sitting majestically atop the ship.

Fifty feet away from the bar were two shirtless men playing backgammon. One shaded his eyes and glanced up at the helicopter. His name was Webb McDonald, sixty years old today, big Trump hair, ten-dollar sunglasses, he could stand to lose a few. He was the owner of the *Miss Adventure.*

The man across from him, mid-fifties, balding and slight, was Florida Senator Charlie Harrow.

Harrow moved his piece on the backgammon board and glanced up at the helicopter. "So where'd the chopper go?" he asked.

"Brigham took it out for a little spin," McDonald said, rolling the dice. "Palm Beach, I think."

Five feet away from them were two men slouched down in deck chairs. Ed Tradd and Ned Betz. Ed and Ned—or Fric and Frac—as Harrow called them behind their backs, were McDonald's longtime bodyguards. Dressed alike in long tan pants and similar black mesh sports shirts, they looked like guys who'd be more at home at the local bowling alley.

Tradd's eyes flicked around like a hawk searching for prey while Betz watched the men play, no clue what the rules of the game were. The butt of an automatic pistol poked out of Betz's waist and a leather strap was visible over Tradd's shoulder. Tradd heard something and his head whipped around.

A man with a Texas-sized grin and a Heineken in one hand crossed the deck. On either side of him walked six women—three on each side. The women were all perfect twelves and dressed in outfits ranging from skimpy to skimpier. McDonald noticed Harrow's eyebrows arch and he turned around.

The man with the Heineken was Bart Brigham, a blond, aging preppy in his forties who gave off a distinct party-hearty vibe. He grinned at McDonald and started singing:

"Happy Birthday to you! Happy Birthday to you! Happy Birthday dear We-ebb! Happy Birth—"

McDonald held up his hand. "Thanks, Brig."

"How do you like your birthday presents?" Brigham asked, then pointed to one of them, "I'd like you to meet Ali"—then to another —"and that's Brett"—then to a third—"and say hello to Diane."

Diane, in a tight, short skirt and a porch full of cleavage, blew McDonald a kiss.

Brigham was not done. "And Brittany, and, ah..." He had no clue.

"Hi...I'm Cassandra," the girl introduced herself.

"And I'm Jess," said the sixth.

She curtsied. A nice touch.

McDonald wasn't thrilled to see the new arrivals but faked it.

Charlie Harrow, on the other hand, judging from the way he was ogling Diane, seemed delighted with the women additions.

"Well, ladies, welcome aboard, you bring bathing suits?" Harrow asked.

Diane pulled up her skirt to reveal a banana peel-sized bikini bottom. Harrow shot her a thumbs-up.

"Come on then, what are you waiting for?" Harrow said, motioning toward the pool. "Hop in, take a dip."

"Catch some rays," Brigham chimed in, draping an arm around Diane's shoulder. "Pound a few cocktails!"

TWO

TEN MILES AWAY, at the Palm Beach International Airport, Clay Terry, a man in his late twenties, strode purposely through the airport. He was clearly a man on a mission. Handsome with close-cropped hair, everything about him looked taut, measured and disciplined. A big smile suddenly lit up his face and his walk turned into a jog.

Alexa McDonald, mid-twenties, razor-sharp cheekbones, a killer smile and dazzling emerald eyes, ran into his arms. He gave her a long kiss on the lips.

"Welcome back, honey," she said, pulling back. "Ten whole days...I'm not letting you out of my sight for one minute."

He touched the tip of her nose. "Don't worry, I'm not going anywhere," he said, then kissed her again like what he was – a soldier on leave.

A kid with a mullet walked past them. "Get a room."

Alexa came up for air. "People really say that?"

At the end of a long wooden dock, in the middle of nowhere, Florida, men with AK-47's, Mac 10's, automatic pistols and darkened faces were climbing into two go-fast boats, a Donzi and a Cigarette. There were twelve of them—guys you'd never mess with.

Rafe Gault, a lean, muscular-looking man with penetrating blue eyes and a cigar butt dangling out of the corner of his mouth, watched the men board the boats. Wearing a sleeveless camouflage T-shirt, tight black jeans and a look of authority, he was clearly the man in charge. Slung over one of his shoulders was a big, elaborate-looking weapon with a five-foot tube, scope and hi-tech antennae. It was a Stinger rocket launcher with the capability of blowing big things into tiny pieces.

Gault's arm was around a sweet-looking, blond-haired boy who appeared to be about ten years old. On the other side of Gault, holding his hand, was a tall, exotic woman. His wife, Catalina.

"Can't I come, Dad?" the little boy asked.

Gault smiled down at him and patted him on the shoulder. "Sorry, bud, you got school."

One hand on the Stinger, he leaned down and kissed his son on the cheek, then his wife, then hopped into the Donzi.

A rail-thin man, with an ear-to-ear scar on his neck, walked to the end of the dock and nodded to Gault. Del Scaletti had the focus and intensity of a cobra ready to strike. A combination M-16 assault rifle and M-203 grenade launcher hung from his shoulder. He flicked his head at Gault's Stinger.

"Just in case the Air Force shows up?" Scaletti said.

Gault just gave him a half nod.

Another man in his late thirties, with a Tyson-like facial tattoo and a Fu Manchu, came down to the dock and, without a word, jumped into the Cigarette. Trash Tatem had a sawed-off shotgun and a burlap bag in one hand, and in the other a metal box with holes in it. Something moved inside the burlap bag.

Gault eyed it.

"Their lunch," Tatem said to Gault. "Barking tree frogs."

"Yummy," Gault said, then signaled the boats' drivers. "All right, boys, let's hit it. We got a bumpy two hours, then jackpot."

THREE

WITH RICH, lustrous mahogany walls and as high tech as it got, the bridge on the *Miss Adventure* had sixteen large, non-glare screens on its Nav-Com panel. Behind it in elevated, padded leather chairs, sat the *Miss Adventure*'s captain and first officer. The owner, Webb McDonald, walked in, nodded to the two, then sat down in an observation area above them. Curt, McDonald's captain, had been with him for fifteen years and they had more than an employer/employee relationship. They'd become good friends.

"Still thinkin' Lyford tomorrow?" Curt asked about their destination in the Bahamas.

"How far is it again?" McDonald asked.

"A hundred-seventy-six nautical miles, to be exact," Curt said studying a map.

"That's a lotta gas for dinner and eighteen holes."

Curt laughed. "Hey, I don't mean to be a wise ass, Webb, but aren't you a little beyond worrying about gas money?"

"Yeah, except I got my little environmentalist daughter lecturing me all the time. Plus, don't forget, I'm a New Englander."

Curt put the map down. "You mean, as in frugal?"

"Hell, no," McDonald said. "As in cheap as shit."

Curt laughed and the first mate joined in.

"Oh, I forgot to tell you," McDonald said, "Alexa told me she has a visitor in town."

No reaction from Curt.

McDonald shook his head. "What the hell's with you two?"

Curt didn't make eye contact. "Come on, Webb, let's not go there."

"You know, you're one hell of a stubborn bastard." McDonald stood up. "I mean, I'd be pretty damn proud—"

Curt raised his hand. Enough.

"Fine," McDonald said, shaking his head and walking away. "Goddamn hard ass."

McDonald had borrowed the design for his casino from the old casino in Monte Carlo, but his was just one-tenth the size. The betting, though, was the same. And if the house won, which it almost always did, McDonald gave the profits to charity. He could afford to.

Harrow and McDonald were at the craps table and two of the women Brigham brought on board were farther down the table. Harrow blew on the dice then flung them the length of the table.

"Niner from Caroliner!" Harrow said.

He crapped out instead and pounded his fist on the side of the table. "Shit."

Tradd and Betz were posted up behind McDonald, trying to blend in. Other men and women were playing at the roulette and blackjack tables nearby.

McDonald glanced down at the two women and said under his breath, "Why'd Brigham have to bring 'em out here? S'posed to be a boys' weekend."

"You know why. Guy thinks with his dick," Harrow said, rolling the dice again. "Eighter from Decatur!"

He shook his head in disgust when he saw he had crapped out again. This time with double ones.

"Double one-er, what a bummer!" McDonald said, pulling a thin card out of his breast pocket.

"Okay, people," McDonald addressed the room, "since the senator is about to go broke, the casino's closing up and the nightclub is about to open its doors."

McDonald pressed the thin card and in a slow, hydraulic whir the craps table, roulette wheel, and blackjack tables disappeared into the floor. He touched it again and—as the women looked on in jaw-drop amazement—sumptuous leather chairs, plush couches, and a full bar rose up out of the floor. In seconds the gaming room was gone, replaced by what looked like an elegant living room in a posh Mayfair townhouse.

"So, ladies... I welcome you to Annabel's, the London club where I met my second wife," McDonald said. "A very costly encounter, I might add."

A guard at the stern of the *Miss Adventure* was looking through a pair of binoculars. He heard footsteps and turned in the direction they came from. Dave Gault, the *Miss Adventure's* second mate, walked toward him.

"Hey, Dave," the guard said. "Nice night."

Dave looked around quickly, then pulled a pistol out of his waistband and shot the guard—point blank—between the eyes. "It was."

The guard toppled over the railing and splashed into the ocean below.

The ersatz Annabel's nightclub was rocking. Everyone was drinking, dancing, carousing. Bart Brigham was pawing three-sheets-to-the-wind Diane, who was nursing a Big Gulp-sized cocktail. McDonald, sitting between Harrow and one of the girls, touched his thin card again. This time a round four-foot-wide platform, sheathed in soft leather, rose noiselessly up out of the floor in the middle of the room.

McDonald stood up. "And for you ladies in the house," he had to practically shout, "we have a very special guest."

He thumbed the thin card again and Justin Timberlake appeared on the platform, singing "My Love."

There was stunned silence for a second. The women couldn't believe their eyes. Then several of them burst into applause. Bra-less Diane dragged Brigham out onto the dance floor. Another couple followed.

Then, a few moments later, Diane, apparently deciding to trade up, sashayed over to the platform and skipped up the three steps to the top. She peeled off her top, threw it to Brigham and started grinding —bare-breasted—next to Justin Timberlake.

His friends shouting their lusty approval, McDonald frowned. He was not thrilled about his high-toned London club being turned into a bawdy strip joint.

Harrow swung around to McDonald. "You love your new toy, don't you?" he said. "One of those hologram things, right?"

McDonald nodded and pressed the card once more. Poof!

Timberlake disappeared and in his place was a curvaceous blonde with her back to the crowd.

"And now," McDonald said, "a special birthday present *from* me *to* me—"

The woman turned and lifted her head. It was, ohmigod, Marilyn. Yes, *the* Marilyn...in a sexy, sheer, sequined number. She started gyrating, as Madonna and Lady Gaga only wished they could. All eyes were trained on the mother-of-all sex symbols. Marilyn looked out at the crowd, then started slowly singing in that famously throaty voice, "Hap-py birth-day, to... you, Hap-py birth-day, to... you—"

The crowd cheered boisterously and sang along. "Happy birth-day, dear We-eb, happy birthday to you."

Harrow turned to McDonald. "Don't suppose you'd care to introduce me?"

McDonald laughed and put the thin card back in his breast pocket. "Are you kidding? Girl doesn't mess around with lowly senators. She's got a date with JFK after here."

FOUR

THE TWO GO-FAST BOATS—THEIR engines cut—silently drifted up to the swimming platform. Gault and his men climbed out and snuck up the steps to the main deck.

Dave was there waiting.

"Welcome aboard," said Dave, a younger, shorter version of his brother, Rafe.

Looking around the boat, Gault nodded.

"You got my email, right?" Dave asked. "The pictures of his bodyguards."

Gault pulled out a few folded-up printouts from his back pocket.

"Yeah, but something on one of your schematic doesn't add up," Gault said, showing the printout to his brother. "Master state room's got a walk-in the size of a fuckin' house."

"Yeah? So?" Dave said. "Dude's got a lotta threads. Plus it's a Feadship. Whaddaya expect?"

The music from McDonald's nightclub in the background cranked up a few decibels.

"I checked out twenty Feadship plans," Gault said. "No walk-ins anywhere near that size."

"Jesus, Rafe, the shit you get hung up on. You check out his awesome Sikorsky chopper?"

"It's not a Sikorsky, it's an Augusta Westland," Gault said, glancing at Del Scaletti next to him. "What do you say, time to go introduce ourselves to our host, don't ya think?"

Scaletti smiled and nodded.

The twelve men crept across the deck to where the music was coming from. Gault held up his hand outside the door and glanced around at his men proudly. He couldn't have assembled a more treacherous-looking band of outlaws, cutthroats and killers.

He nodded and they all burst into the nightclub with an arsenal of raised automatic weapons.

"Hit the deck!" Gault yelled, his eyes flashing around the room. "Everybody on the floor."

Then he spotted Tradd and Betz. Tradd was yanking a Glock from his shoulder holster and Betz was reaching for a pistol jammed into his pants.

But Gault was too fast. He swung his Uzzi at them and fired off two short bursts.

Tradd and Betz crashed backwards as Gault motioned to Trash Tatem.

"Go get the captain," Gault yelled, then glancing over at another one of his men, Reg King. "Take five guys, round up the crew."

King, a baby-faced man wearing a backward Yankee's baseball cap, nodded and signaled five men to follow him.

Gault's eyes scanned to his left and landed on McDonald. He smiled triumphantly at seeing the stunned and grim-faced McDonald, then walked toward him.

"Get everyone's cell phones," he said to Scaletti, then leaned close to McDonald. "Gimme yours."

McDonald handed him his iPhone.

"Thanks, bro," Gault said. "Hey, I been just dyin' to meetcha."

McDonald didn't react.

Gault noticed Brittany standing next to McDonald and bowed. "And who might you be, Sunshine?"

Brittany didn't crack a smile. "Brittany," she said, frostily.

"*Enchante*," Gault said.

Brittany was not charmed.

Gault glanced over at Charlie Harrow, on the other side of McDonald. "And Charlie Harrow, what an honor," he said. "Even though I voted for the other guy. Not real big on that gun control policy of yours."

Harrow smiled nervously.

"Okay, boys and girls," Gault said, raising his voice, "don't make me shoot anyone else. Do what I say and you can get back to your fun and games in no time."

Judging by their terrified looks, no one bought that.

Del Scaletti, his knapsack stuffed full of cell phones, came up to Gault, who was eyeballing McDonald top to bottom. "Know something," Gault said to McDonald, "you're my role model. Dirt poor growing up, scratch up a few bucks, buy yourself a coupla motels, wheel and deal, and boom, by age sixty you got it all… billionaire... big ass boat... Happy Birthday, by the way, Weeb."

"It's Webb."

Gault just scratched his three-day-old facial growth. "So now, question is, the most important deal of your life... are you gonna get it done or fuck it up?"

McDonald just stared back at him.

Scaletti took a quick step forward and jabbed McDonald in the gut with his Uzzi. "That was not a rhetorical question, big mon," Scaletti said.

McDonald doubled over in pain.

Barely suppressed amusement appeared on Gault's face. "Sorry, my business associate's got kind of a hair trigger," he said. "Big vocabulary, though, for a seventh-grade dropout."

Scaletti beamed with pride.

"So talk to me, Weeb," Gault said.

"About what?" McDonald asked, gasping and clutching his stomach.

"Something along the lines of, 'what kinda deal did you have in mind, Rafe?'"

"All right," McDonald said with a grimace, "what kind of—"

"Thanks for asking," Gault said. "Word is you just stroked a nice, fat check to wife number two. Three hundred million, according to Forbes. So how 'bout we pretend, just for fun, I'm wife number three, and, sadly, it didn't work out—"

"Yeah, irreconcilable differences," Scaletti said, shooting Gault an off-kilter grin.

"And now I want *my* three hundred mil," Gault said. "Which we all know is chump change for a big swingin' dick like you, seeing how you're worth eight billion."

McDonald gave Gault a look like he must be sniffing glue. "Are you out of your mind? No way I can get my hands on that kind of money. It'd take months."

"Come on, Weeb, that's bullshit and you know it," Gault said, shaking his head. "You got 'til Wednesday at five."

"That's insane, it's impossible."

Gault shook his head slowly. "All those articles I read about you being such a can-do kinda guy. It's just Sunday night, you got plenty of time." Gault looked over at Harrow. "What do you say, Senator?"

Harlow's lip was quivering. "I-I might be able to help out... financially, I mean."

Gault clapped him on the back. "Look at that, Del," Gault said to Scaletti. "That's the kinda spirit we like to see."

"Very magnanimous," Scaletti said, nodding. "A real team player."

FIVE

RENALDO'S WAS A NICE, white tablecloth restaurant in Palm Beach, but not one favored by the ultra-rich or super chic. Which was exactly why Alexa and Clay were there. Clay, dressed in a blue blazer over a sport shirt, was holding Alexa's hand. She was wearing a black skirt and a beige silk top.

"Pulled the old blazer out of mothballs," Clay said, tugging at the lapel.

"Little tight on you," Alexa said. "But very Palm Beach-y."

"Oh, yeah, that's me," Clay said with a laugh.

"Hey, there are worse things than Palm Beach-y."

"Oh, yeah? Such as?"

"Well…such as Saint Barts-y?"

He laughed. "Christ, spare me."

She leaned across and kissed him. "God, I missed you," she said. "So catch me up on what you're doing over there? You know, stuff you won't have to kill me after you tell me."

"Same old, same old...sand and turbans."

She took a sip of her wine. "Come on, you never tell me anything. It's really kind of annoying."

"Sorry," he said, patting her hand, "but that's pretty much the job description."

Alexa took a sip of her Pinot Grigio. "You gonna call your dad while you're here?"

"Nope."

Alexa shook her head. "Don't you think it's time you two kissed and made up?"

"Much rather kiss you," Clay said, leaning in and doing just that.

"You truly are a master of changing the subject," Alexa said, as the waiter delivered their dinners. "I suppose we're going to talk about the weather next."

Clay eyed his lamb chops. "Man, I missed food like this over there."

"There's an easy solution to that, you know."

Gault handed McDonald's cell phone to him. "Time to start dialin' for dollars, old buddy," he said.

"Who am I calling?" McDonald asked.

"The Executive VP of McDonald International," Gault said.

McDonald hesitated too long for Gault. Gault raised the Uzzi and pressed it up against McDonald's jowly cheek, his tone turning sadistic. "You gotta get a lot quicker on the uptake, bro," he said, grabbing McDonald's cheek. "I say jump, you jump."

McDonald nodded reluctantly.

Gault pointed at McDonald's phone. "Dial the fuckin' thing!"

McDonald started to dial, then looked up at Gault. "I can have fifty million wired tomorrow."

Gault's eyebrow arched. "Yeah, and the other two fifty?"

Sweat poured off McDonald's forehead. His silence said fifty million was all he was offering.

Gault raised his Uzzi up to McDonald's face again. "Open up."

McDonald opened his mouth. Gault jammed his Uzzi in it. "You just ain't gettin' it, man. You may be a hell of a negotiator, but I ain't negotiating. I'm tellin'." Gault's eyes narrowed. "You got to the count of three to tell me how much you're getting' me. One...two..."

"Tweee-hun-dwed-miwwion," Came McDonald's garbled response through the muzzle of the Uzzi.

Gault glanced at Scaletti and snickered. "How much?"

Scaletti laughed. "He said, 'twee-hun-dwed-miwwion."

Gault smiled and looked back at McDonald. "You're not light in the loafers, by any chance, are you, Weeb?"

Scaletti snorted a laugh.

"And when am I getting my twee-hun-dwed miwwion?" Gault demanded.

"Weds-dee," said McDonald.

"Now we're talkin'. But wiring it, my friend, ain't gonna happen. I want it in my hot little hands. Cash money."

Gault pointed at Scaletti's knapsack. "Got that K-bar in your bag of tricks, Del?"

Scaletti nodded, reached back in his knapsack and pulled out a K-bar knife.

Gault walked toward McDonald and raised the knife. McDonald's eyes bulged and sweat ran down his flushed cheeks.

"Relax, I'm not gonna hurt you. It's just that hairdo. It's buggin' the shit out of me," Gault said. "That picture of you on the cover of Forbes. I mean, come on, man! Your damn hair looked worse than the fuckin' Donald's."

"*You're fired!*" Scaletti said, grinning and jabbing a finger at McDonald.

Gault grabbed a clump of McDonald's hair and cut it off. McDonald looked terrified.

"For Chrissakes, what—"

"I said relax," Gault said. "A little on this side... a little on that."

McDonald's hair fell to the floor. He looked totally helpless. His friends and the women watched in stunned silence. Gault's men, on the other hand, sported knowing half-smiles, like they'd seen their boss's performances before and were huge fans.

Gault finished cutting. It was a crude Mohawk.

Scaletti put his hand up to his mouth and started whooping like a wild Indian. “Woo-woo-woo-woo!”

Gault chuckled and handed McDonald the phone. “O-kay, now dial the damn thing.”

SIX

ALEXA AND CLAY were having dessert. Alexa took a sip of an after-dinner drink. Clay had a half-filled beer glass in front of him.

Alexa's phone rang. She glanced down, hit the red button, and looked back up at Clay.

"Dad... out on the boat with all the usual suspects." She put her hand on his. "Sure you don't want to see Curt?"

Clay shook his head emphatically.

Alexa stroked his cheek. "It's so stupid, just because of some dumb DWI and a night in the slammer."

Clay scratched the back of his head nervously.

"Ah, actually, two nights in the slammer…and"—he coughed—"driving a stolen car."

"Oh, my bad. Guess I only got half the story."

"That's 'cause I never told you the whole thing. Didn't want you thinking I was a one-man crime spree."

"Okay, so give me all the gory details."

"Well," Clay sighed, "it started out as a beer run at my buddies' house. Problem was I was too drunk to tell the difference between his Matrix and his neighbor's Lexus. So I got into the Lexus, went down to the Seven Eleven and backed into a fire hydrant—"

"Oops."

"Then a cop showed up and I called him an *expletive deleted*, which was right after I sideswiped a pot belly palm, and right before they threw me in the drunk tank."

Nodding, Alexa took another sip of her drink. "So let me get this straight. Grand theft auto, verbal cop abuse… did you, by any chance, hold up a bank?"

Clay smiled, but looked sheepish.

"Never got around to that, but while I'm coming clean, there were a few other... infractions."

Alexa leaned closer. "Okay, so spill it."

"Well, for one thing I got busted," Clay said, reaching for his glass and taking a quick sip. "Once for dealing—"

"Jesus, Clay, you were a serious badass."

"Which was really just selling a few bags to friends." Clay's jaw tightened. "Then the old man threw me out of the house. Can't say I blame him, hardly a model son. But saying I was somehow responsible for the trouble between Mom and him, that was *way, way* over the top."

"Yeah, totally. How can an eighteen year old—"

"I know... so after a while he called me up, tried to apologize."

Alexa leaned forward and put her hand on his. "What'd you say?"

"Hung up on him."

Alexa threw her hands up in the air.

"You know, you're both a couple of rock heads."

Clay was squirming. "Okay, let's change the subject. How 'bout we talk about—"

"Us?" Alexa said.

Clay smiled but still looked uneasy. "You know where that always goes."

"Yeah, 'cause you've drilled it into my head a million times," Alexa said. "We get married, you step on a land mine, I'm a widow."

"That and the fact we'd still be seven thousand miles apart."

Alexa wiped her mouth with her napkin. "Just so happens, I talked to Dad and he's open to me scouting new hotel locations in Delhi and Dubai?"

"Not exactly right around the corner from Bagram."

"Hey, it's not so far. We could meet halfway on weekends."

He leaned across and kissed her. "I love you, honey, and how your mind works—"

"Don't you *dare* say 'but.'"

"But…did I mention how hot you look?"

Alexa laughed. "A couple times."

"Good, 'cause I meant it."

The waiter came over and started clearing their plates. Clay drained the rest of his beer.

"Get you folks another drink?"

Alexa looked up at him and smiled. "No, thanks."

Clay shook his head.

"Gotta watch out for this guy," Alexa said. "Does crazy things if he has one too many."

SEVEN

MCDONALD WAS TRYING to ease the tension. Telling his friends and the six girls that everything was going to be all right. Judging by the looks on their faces, he wasn't having much success.

It was 11:30 now and McDonald and the others had been herded into one side of the large aft fantail salon. Curt Terry and his crew were separated from them on the other side of the salon. Gault and his men were guarding them.

Sitting on a brown leather couch, Harrow whispered to McDonald, "Guy's just working third grade intimidation tactics. He can't do anything to you, you're his meal ticket. That cutting Samson's hair routine, I mean, Jesus, gimme a break."

"Yeah, I know," McDonald said, sneaking Harrow his thin remote control card. "Here, take this. I don't want Gault finding it on me."

Gault, across the room, noticed them talking. "Something you boys want to share with the class?"

"No," McDonald said, "just saying how much I like my new haircut."

"Yeah, well, you're lookin' good, bro," Gault said. "Try your daughter again."

"I just did."

"Well, call her the fuck again," Gault said, boiling over. "Call her every two minutes 'til you get her." Then a smile. "Guess you folks can tell, I'm not a very patient man."

Gault motioned to Scaletti, who followed him over to a wall nearby. Gault flipped a switch. "Check this out," he said, pointing.

On the starboard side of the room, the floor opened up and a large dumbwaiter whirred up out of it.

Scaletti nodded, impressed. Gault pushed another switch. A fully stocked bar came up out of the floor on the port side.

"Thirsty?" Gault asked.

"Yeah," Scaletti said with a smile, "I could use a libation. A little shot of Jack would hit the spot right about now."

Gault shook his head. "Sorry, man, you're on the job," he said. "Hey, by the way, where the hell is King?"

Clay put the key into the door of Alexa's house while he kissed her, holding back nothing. Alexa shoved the door open with her back, then kicked off her shoes in the foyer.

Clay worked his jacket off, then let it fall to the floor. "You don't know how many nights I fell asleep on my little cot at Bagram, rehearsing this scene."

Alexa laughed and pulled his shirt over his head as he fumbled with her bra underneath her top. He unclipped it, then let it drop.

"And you have no idea how many nights I dreamed of... ripping your clothes off," she said.

"Well, rip away," he said.

She put a hand on a button of his blue jeans and fumbled around trying to unbutton it. She finally got it open, then went for his zipper. But instead she found a row of metal buttons. She looked up at him, frustrated.

"You didn't have any trouble last time," he said.

She laughed. "Come on, gimme a hand here, soldier boy?"

Clay whipped through the snap buttons, then put his arms around Alexa's back and kissed her—bare chest to bare chest. They were backed up against a large snow-white sofa. In mid-kiss, she reached back, felt the sofa behind her and sat down on the side of it. She leaned back slowly and Clay followed her as they both fell onto the sofa.

"Nice trust fall," he said.

Alexa's phone rang.

She looked down at the number. "Goddammit, Daddy, leave me alone. I'm... busy."

EIGHT

THE FIRST OFFICER of the *Miss Adventure*, Matt Steiner, came stealing out of the night shadows, one arm around the neck of Gault's man, Reg King. He had a pistol pressed up against King's head.

Gault looked up and saw Steiner shuffling toward him.

"Okay, all of you, guns on the deck," Steiner shouted.

All twelve heavily armed men looked over at Gault. Gault, not looking particularly distressed, just stared at Steiner.

"Sorry, Rafe," Reg King said, "I fucked up. Went into the engine room, this guy was in there— hiding out with his piece."

"Hey, no sweat, Reg, we all make mistakes," Gault said. "Okay, boys, you heard the man. Lay down your guns."

Gault put down his Uzzi and it looked like he was going to do the same with a pistol tucked into his waistband. Instead he jerked it up suddenly and shot King point blank in the face. Blood splattered Steiner as King fell hard to the deck.

"Just don't fuck up on my time, okay, Reg?" Gault said, then he eyed Steiner. "Looks like you just lost your bargaining chip, pal."

Gault's men picked up their guns. "And 'cause you tried to be a hero, one of my guys is dead," Gault said. "Old Reg had a girlfriend and three kids. My guess is they'd want your scalp. Drop the gun, partner."

Steiner didn't hesitate.

"Wise decision. I appreciate your effort to avert further bloodshed," Gault said earnestly.

He looked around, then motioned to Trash Tatem. Tatem came over and Gault whispered something in his ear. Tatem smiled, nodded, then walked away.

Then Gault flicked a glance over at another one of his men, Ron Jon.

Ron Jon, long, ratty blond hair and a loud, surfer shirt, came over to Gault.

Gault whispered a command and Ron Jon's face lit up. He nodded and headed toward the stern of the boat.

Twenty feet away, Gault saw McDonald whisper something to Harrow. "Kind of rude... you and all your secrets, Weeb."

McDonald looked like he had been caught in the act. "I just said, may God have mercy on the soul of Mr. King, was all."

Gault nodded. "That's a very touching sentiment, Weeb." Gault bowed his head. "I'd like y'all to join me now in a prayer for the soul of Reg King—" he closed his eyes— "Lord..."

All of Gault's men bowed their heads. "Lord," they said in unison.

Gault continued. "Lord, we ask you to sanctify the life of your obedient servant, Reg King."

Gault's men repeated after him. "Lord, we ask you to sanctify the life of your obedient servant, Reg King."

Gault glared at McDonald. "I can't hear you, Weeb," he said, then continuing. "Reg was a man of grace, courage, and quiet dignity. Lord have mercy on his soul."

This time McDonald joined in with Gault's men. "Reg was a man of grace, courage, and quiet dignity. Lord have mercy on his soul."

"Amen," said Gault.

"Amen," said Gault's men and McDonald.

At the stern of the *Miss Adventure*, Trash Tatem stepped down into one of the go-fast boats tied to the swimming platform. He lifted a white twenty-gallon bucket out of the starboard side of the boat and got back onto the *Miss Adventure.*

He walked back up, across the deck, then between Gault's men and the crew, carrying the bucket. He went over to the port rail, stuck a wooden ladle into the bucket and came up with a batch of bloody chum. Then he tossed it into the sea below.

Clay was looking up at the ceiling. Alexa, naked beside him, had her head propped up on one elbow, a big smile on her face.

"You gonna see what your old man thinks is so important?" Clay asked.

Alexa got up, went over to her purse, and pulled out her cell. "Guess I should, now that I'm not distracted anymore."

"Oh, so that's what you call it?"

She laughed, dialed, then hit the green button.

An unfamiliar voice answered. "Hello?"

"Who's this?" Alexa said.

There was a pause. "Jack Sparrow," said the voice.

"I want to talk to my father, Webb McDonald," Alexa said, frowning.

"'Bout time you checked in, Alexa. How's tricks at 915 Banyan Road?"

Her frown got larger. "Put my father on."

Gault handed the phone to McDonald. "Bossy little bitch."

"Hi, honey," McDonald said.

"What's wrong, Dad, who was that—"

"Guess you didn't listen to my message."

Gault grabbed the phone out of McDonald's hand. "Enough of the chitchat. Look, honey, let me draw you a picture: I got twelve men on

Daddy's boat. And I'm not talking nice, genteel men, but heavily armed, stone cold killers." He eyed his men and broke into a wide smile of pride. They grinned back at him. "And, honey, as sick as it may sound, they love the sight of blood. So unless I get three hundred million dollars in unmarked hundreds by Wednesday at five, we gonna have a boatload of dead fat cats out here. Oh and sweetheart, we're talking slow and gruesome. My business associate has a blowtorch and a power drill. Get the picture? So I suggest you make a trip to your bank nice and early tomorrow morning."

Gault clicked off.

He looked over and saw Ron Jon walk toward Trash Tatem, who was ladling more chum into the ocean.

On Ron Jon's left shoulder was the eight-foot-long diving board, which he had removed from the pool. Ron Jon took it with both hands and set it down on the deck so it cantilevered out over the edge of the boat.

Del Scaletti walked up to him, pulled out a hammer and four long spikes from his knapsack and handed them to Ron Jon. Ron Jon nodded to him, got down in a crouch, held one of the spikes on top of the diving board and started hammering. Then he did the same with the other three spikes.

"What the hell's he doing?" McDonald asked.

"What's it look like?" Gault said, signaling to Scaletti.

Using his foot, Scaletti shoved Matt Steiner over to Gault.

"So, my friend," Gault turned to Steiner, "life lesson number one —you gotta own your shit."

Steiner put his hands up. "Hey, man, I got two kids—"

Gault cut him off. "Like I told you, my man Reg had three. How 'bout you just man up. None of that begging for mercy shit, huh?"

Gault looked over at McDonald. "Yo, Weeb, dial up my girlfriend again."

McDonald's eyes narrowed and his fists tightened.

"Do it," Gault hissed.

Cell phone in hand, Alexa paced her living room, wearing a white robe and a king-size frown. Clay was sneaking a look through the living room curtains, a pair of binoculars up to his eyes. Alexa's cell phone rang.

She punched the green button on her cell.

"Dad?"

Clay walked over and put his head close to the phone. "Nope. Jack Sparrow again. I want to set the stage for you, doll. Your father's first officer's rash action led to the death of one of my men. So now, in a rather crude and—"

Gault glanced over at Scaletti.

"Antiquated," said Scaletti.

"Yeah, in a rather crude and antiquated form of justice, the first officer is gonna walk the plank."

Gault looked over at the crew and captain standing in a more or less straight line, trying to suck it up and look stoical. They were facing the port side of the boat. Gault's uniformed brother, Dave, was standing in the middle of the crew. Captain Curt Terry was standing erect, his brow creased with lines and looking as though he was struggling mightily to hold himself back. Then without warning, he suddenly started walking toward Gault.

But Scaletti headed him off, thrusting his Uzzi up against Terry's chest. "Whoa, whoa, Cap, where ya think you're goin'?"

Gault noticed. "Hang on a sec, doll," he said into his cell phone. "The captain's acting up."

Terry pushed Scaletti's gun away. "I want to talk to him."

Scaletti's eyes flicked over to Gault. Gault nodded. "You've been granted an audience," Scaletti said.

Terry walked over to Gault, Scaletti right behind him.

Gault smiled at him. "So what's up, Cap?"

"My First Officer didn't do a damn thing. I want you to let him go."

Gault looked at Scaletti and they both started laughing.

"Oh, do you now?" Gault said. "And based on what authority? 'Cause you steer the fuckin' boat and know how to read charts? 'Cause of those little stripes and bars on your shirt?"

Terry eyeballed him with extreme malice.

Gault took a step closer, their eyes six inches apart. "Well, listen up and listen good, fuckhead. I got the guns and I got the bullets and where I come from that outranks captains and admirals any day of the week."

Gault shoved him backwards. Terry started to come at him, but thought better of it. He turned and walked away, his head not as high as it was before.

"Go back to your crew," Gault said. "Maybe they'll take you a little more seriously."

Dave Gault walked over to Terry, put his arm on his shoulder, comfortingly, and guided him back to the rest of the crew.

A tiny flicker of amusement crept across Gault's face.

McDonald and his friends watched from the nearby section of the deck. They looked jittery, agitated and terrified, not ready for the next chapter to unfold, as they watched Scaletti and Trash Tatem lash the First Officer's hands behind his back with plastic ties. Then they wrapped duct tape around his eyes and shoved him toward the diving board.

Gault raised the cell back up to his mouth. "I'm back, doll," he said to Alexa. "Sorry, the captain was getting all macho on me," then cranking up his best Marv Albert. "Okay, so back to the action: The First Officer is being led to the port side of the boat."

Steiner stopped walking. "No!" he cried out.

Scaletti shoved him roughly toward the rail.

"He's just a few steps from the plank now," Gault said into his cell.

Steiner was whimpering quietly now. Gault and his men laughed, as Ron Jon recorded the action with his cell phone. Scaletti reached into his knapsack and pulled out two cattle prods. He handed one to

Ron Jon, who put his phone in his pocket, then the other to Tatem. Gault shot Scaletti an approving nod.

"Got everything in there you need?" Gault said.

"Hey, 'be prepared,' ya know," Scaletti said. "My old boy scout training comes in handy."

Scaletti and Ron Jon, on either side of Steiner, zapped him toward the plank. Steiner accidentally put his foot on it while Tatem and Ron Jon zapped him a few more times. Scaletti threw another load of chum into the water. A shark's fin ominously glided by and the shark snapped at the chum.

"Still there, doll?" Gault asked Alexa.

He listened, then frowned at Scaletti.

"She just called me a nasty name, Del."

"Okay, okay, message received," Alexa said into the phone. "What are you trying to prove? Let him go."

"First the captain, now you," Gault said, shaking his head and looking at Scaletti. "All these people trying to give me orders. Hey, I'd really like to accommodate you, doll, but there's something called—" he glanced at Scaletti.

"Retribution," Scaletti said.

"Yeah," Gault said. "So permission denied."

Scaletti and Ron Jon had zapped the First Officer halfway onto the plank.

"The First Officer's on the plank now," Gault said softly.

Ron Jon zapped him hard and flashed a psycho grin.

"The First Officer takes a jolt to the left shoulder," Gault said, watching Ron Jon zap him again, "and another one to the gut. He's back on his heels now."

Trash Tatem zapped him. "A shot to the back," Gault said, getting animated. "And another one to his hip. He's staggering back now, he's…" Steiner, arms wind milling, let out a bloodcurdling scream.

"Man overboard. There's a big splash, he comes back up to the surface, he screams, there's blood everywhere... he's, he's—"

Flashing sharks teeth, bloody, roiling water.

"Shark bait!" Gault shouted.

Gault just watched for a few moments. "And that's the end of our live broadcast. Hope you enjoyed the show, girlfriend. Remember to get with your banker first thing tomorrow morning." He clicked off with her and walked over to McDonald and his friends as if nothing had happened. He looked around, taking satisfaction in their horrified expressions.

"Okay, boys and girls, the show's over. It's two in the morning. Bedtime. We're going to have a very busy day tomorrow. I want everyone sleeping in the fantail. My men were kind enough to go to your cabins and round up a bunch of pillows and blankets. Of course, we have three extra sets of both, compliments of those brave but foolish men who sacrificed their lives earlier. The two bodyguards, who were a little slow on the draw, and the noble first mate. Nighty night, everyone."

He took a few steps toward a mahogany wall in the aft salon, then motioned to Scaletti. "Gimme the K-bar," he said.

Scaletti reached into his knapsack and handed him the knife he had used to cut McDonald's hair.

Gault carved three big Xs into the mahogany wall.

Fifteen minutes later, Gault was leaning over the starboard rail next to the diving board smoking a Cuban. Scaletti, standing next to him had a Marlboro dangling from his mouth. They looked like two men enjoying a relaxing cruise.

"I spoke to the Columbian," Gault said.

Scaletti scowled. The name killed his mood.

"Yeah, what did that scumbag have to say?"

"Hey, Del, don't go getting all personal."

Scaletti laughed sarcastically.

"You mean, just 'cause the little beaner slashed my fuckin' throat?"

"Hey, you lived, didn't you?" Gault said. "Besides it was ten years ago. Before he took over from Pablo. You gotta get over it, let bygones be bygones."

Scaletti shook his head and flicked his butt into the dark sea below.

"Fuckin' Pablo... another sweetheart," he said. "So what'd Ernesto have to say?"

"He wants it," Gault said.

"Well, of course he wants it," Scaletti said. "It's the eighth largest yacht in the fuckin' world."

"Seventh," Gault said, tapping the ash off his Cuban. "I told him I'd give him a really good deal for it. Seventy-five mil. That's like a ninety per cent off fire sale."

"Bet the little prick still tried to hondle you?"

"Yeah, but I told him that was my bottom line," Gault said, "Fact is, I woulda gone lower. I mean, ain't no easy trick unloading a stolen yacht half the size of Rhode Island."

Scaletti ran his hand through his scraggly hair. "Guy's gonna have half the Navy and Coast Guard up his ass when he tries to get it back to Columbia."

"Well, now, that's his problem, isn't it, Del?" Gault said. "Told me he's gonna keep it at that little island he owns. Says he'll be all right as long as he doesn't take it into American waters. Sonavabitch has a big set of cajones on him, I'll give him that."

"Gonna have to build himself a big ass dock," Scaletti said.

"Told me he might keep it in Monte Carlo."

"Monte Carlo?"

"Yeah, he's got a house there."

Scaletti chuckled and shook his head. "Little beaner's doin' all right for himself," he said as the moonlight caught his mossy colored teeth.

"Yeah, once we're done with this job you can buy a house in Monte Carlo too. Look out over the Med... be his neighbor."

Scaletti laughed, spat over the side, and wiped his mouth. "Nah, I'm thinking Lake Como. Right next to my man, George Clooney."

NINE

CLAY WAS CROUCHED DOWN behind a ficus hedge in Alexa's back yard. He watched the man across the street in a black Jeep strike a match and light a cigarette. He had a salt-and-pepper beard and ferret-like eyes. He took a long drag on his cigarette and exhaled.

Staying low and shielded by the hedge, Clay snuck up to the back of the Jeep. He looked around and—noiselessly—took a few steps onto a neighbor's driveway and pried loose a paving stone. Staying down so he couldn't be spotted in a rearview mirror, he inched his way back behind the Jeep again. Then, on all fours, he crawled up to the front door of the Jeep, reached his left hand up to the Jeep's door handle and slowly pushed the lock in. It was locked.

Without hesitating, he stood up and slammed the paving stone through the window, then reached in and popped the lock. The man raised his right arm. He had a gun. Through the broken window, Clay slashed at his wrist with his fist. There was a loud, sickening snap. The man's wrist dropped limply, the gun fell to the floor.

Clay yanked open the door with his left hand and slammed his fist into the man's jaw. The man cried out so loud Clay was afraid he'd wake the neighbors. Clay reached down for the man's gun, grabbed it, and pressed it up against his cheekbone.

"Tell me about your friends on the boat."

"The fuck you talking about?" the man said, wincing in pain. "You broke my goddamn wrist."

Clay pushed the gun into his cheekbone and yanked him out of the car by his collar. He pointed to Alexa's house. "No problem. Got a nurse inside."

Clay followed the man down the driveway to Alexa's front door, then shoved him inside. Alexa was on a couch staring off into space. She hopped up and eyed him like he was covered in maggots.

"So this is our spy?" she asked.

Clay nodded.

Alexa saw his hand hanging loosely.

"What happened to his hand?"

"He stumbled, took a nasty fall."

"Aw, poor baby," Alexa said.

The man shot her a spiteful look.

"Okay, pal, let's start with your name," Clay said.

"Joe Dirk."

"Okay, Joe," Clay said, "here's how we're gonna play it. First, you're gonna sit down."

He motioned with the pistol and Dirk sat in a chair.

"Next, you're gonna give us answers," Clay said. "And if I don't like 'em, I got a surprise for you."

Dirk shifted in his chair.

"Okay, now, tell us about your boss," Clay said.

Dirk's eyes just darted around the room, but he kept silent.

Clay stood up and gestured with his pistol. "Okay, get up, asshole."

Dirk got up and Clay shoved him roughly toward a door. Clay opened the door and pushed Dirk inside Alexa's kitchen. They went through it to a room behind. It was a laundry room and had an oversized, commercial washer and dryer. "I'm sure you're familiar with the concept of water boarding, huh, Joe?"

Clay didn't wait for an answer.

"Well, this is my version of it," Clay said, motioning to the washer. "Get in!"

Dirk's eyes flashed panic.

"Last guy came out spotless."

Dirk raised his arms. "Okay, okay. What do you want to know?"

Clay stared him down for a few moments. "I don't have time to waste. This is your last warning. Next time you're takin' a ride."

Clay motioned with his pistol to the door to the living room.

Clay followed Dirk as they walked out of the laundry room, through the kitchen and back into the living room. Dirk sat down and Clay stayed on his feet.

"So, one more time, tell me about your boss," Clay said. "What's his name?"

"Gault," Dirk said. "Rafe Gault."

"What's he do?"

"Runs drugs down in the Keys. A major player. Going for the big score this time."

"Keep goin'," Clay said.

"People who get in his way usually don't end up breathing so good."

That was something Alexa didn't want to hear. She took three quick steps toward him and slapped him hard across the face.

He shot daggers back at her.

"How many guys with Gault?" Clay asked.

"Twelve including him."

Clay thought for a second. "Okay, tomorrow morning you're gonna call Gault and tell him Alexa went to the bank first thing and is working hard on getting the money. Got it?"

Dirk nodded.

"Another thing, you and I are gonna take a little ride out to the boat together."

"You out of your fuckin' mind?" Dirk said. "That's the last place you wanna go."

"I really want to meet this guy," Clay said, circling Dirk like a shark. "Keep talkin'."

Dirk thought for a few seconds. Too long for Clay. Clay motioned with his pistol. "Come on, fuckhead, time to go for a ride in the Maytag."

Dirk's arms shot up. "For Chrissakes, I don't know what you're asking."

"Everything there is to know about Gault. An up close and personal."

"Well, he grew up in the Keys, been runnin' dope since he was a kid."

"Ever do any time?"

"Nah," Dirk said. "Never got caught."

"Maybe knows who to pay."

"Maybe."

"What else?"

"That's all I know," Dirk said, "'cept the guy's a little crazy."

"What do you mean?"

"I mean, sometimes crazy like a fox. Sometimes crazy like a… lunatic."

TEN

CLAY TUCKED in Joe Dirk for the night, then went up to Alexa's bedroom. She lived in a four-bedroom, four-bathroom house. "*For my future kids,*" she told her friends. It had an elevator and a pool but was fairly modest by Palm Beach standards.

Clay walked in and found her face down on her bed.

She turned and looked up at him. Her eyes were red and she had been crying.

"You all right, honey?"

"Yeah, I'm okay," she said. "What'd you do with our hostage?"

"Stuck him in the elevator and killed the power between floors. It makes for a nice little jail cell. Sure you're okay?"

Alexa forced a smile and nodded.

Clay walked over to the bed. "Turn over," he said.

She did. Then he straddled her and started rubbing her shoulders.

"Oh, God, yes, that's exactly what I need," she said. "A little lower."

"I wouldn't worry about Webb. He's a tough old bastard," he said. "So's my old man."

Clay put his hand on her cheek and stroked it gently.

"I remember my mom and me going out to see Dad on the *Miss*."

He leaned down and kissed her cheek. "That was the first time I ever laid eyes on you. I remember thinking you were a bratty little snob with a mouth full of metal."

She turned and looked up at him. "I thought you were cute."

"I was... a cute little pain in the ass."

Alexa laughed as Clay rubbed her back.

"I really think we should call the police," Alexa said. "Dad's tight with the commissioner."

Clay shook his head. "No way. Guys like Gault, the second they suspect someone's after 'em, they kill all the witnesses."

"But—"

Clay cut her off. "How much can you come up with?"

"In three days? Best case, like a hundred and fifty million. Maybe a little more. Dad's just not liquid right now. He just put up close to a billion for a start-up, plus the divorce."

Clay kneaded her back deeper and smiled. "Where guys like me and Gault come from, that's still a lot of money."

"I still think," Alexa paused, "we should go to the police."

"You got floor plans for the boat?"

"You're ignoring me, Clay."

"I heard you."

"You're not serious about going out there?"

"It is what I do, you know."

"Yeah, but there's twelve of 'em."

"Sounds like a fair fight to me."

"Seriously?"

Clay sighed deeply. "Lex, our options are pretty limited here."

ELEVEN

IT WAS seven thirty the next morning. Gault was on his cell phone looking over the side of the *Miss Adventure*.

"You finish up that science project, bud?"

He listened, then nodded. "Sam, you remember our deal. You ace it and we go out on the boat and catch a swordfish when I come back."

He listened.

"No excuses—" he looked at his watch—"you got an hour and a half before the bus comes."

He listened.

"I miss you too, Sam-bo. Now get to work, buddy."

Gault walked into the fantail salon, a wide grin on his face. Scaletti was right beside him. Forty people were scattered around the fantail salon—on the floor and in couches and chairs—in various sleeping positions. The few who were awake squinted up at him as if they had just wandered into a bad dream.

"All right, everybody, rise and shine. Beautiful day on the high seas. And, 'cause I wanna show you nothing's changed, 'cept, of course, you got a new captain, we gonna start you off with a nice, hearty breakfast. Then recess. Nice calm, flat seas, a great day for water skiing."

People were rubbing their eyes and listening warily to Gault.

McDonald shot an ominous look at Harrow as Gault walked out of the salon.

"Okay, people," Scaletti said, "head on over to the dumbwaiter. We got bacon and eggs, waffles and pancakes, whatever your little hearts desire."

The dumbwaiter whirred up and opened. On three serving platters was a huge selection of breakfast foods. A line of people queued up, plates in hand. They all looked around at each other furtively, as though they didn't want to make eye contact. As if they didn't want to see the terror in each other's eyes.

Alexa and Clay were in bed. He was awake, staring down at floor plans spread out at the end of the bed. Alexa's eyes opened, then almost immediately a frown appeared, as if she suddenly flashed to the reality of last night's events.

"I couldn't really sleep. Could you?" she asked.

"Nah, just been thinking."

"About what?"

Clay smiled and leaned back to her and kissed her.

"Best way to get on the *Miss.*"

"Oh, God, are you really serious about going out there?"

"It's the only thing I see that could work."

She pulled back. "How 'bout going out there with a bunch of other men?"

"'Cause they'd see us coming," Clay said. "A lot more people would end up like the First Officer."

Alexa sat up in bed. "Wait a minute, I just remembered something. Dad built this panic room off the master stateroom."

Clay's eyes lit up. "Jesus, Lex, that makes it a whole new ball game."

Clay's mind immediately started spooling out a plan.

"Problem is," Alexa said, "we don't even know where the *Miss* is."

"I can find out from Dirk," Clay said, looking at his watch. It was 7:15.

"I'm gonna get him up," Clay said. "Have him call Gault, tell him you're on the case. All set to head down to the bank."

Gault and Scaletti stood on the starboard side of the *Miss Adventure* looking out at the ocean. In between them was Webb McDonald. There were deep ruts in his forehead and his eyes were slitty, like he'd rather be anywhere else than wedged between these two miscreants.

Gault had his trademark black Havana stogie hanging out of the left side of his mouth.

"If your little girl loves you, man, she's getting ready to go see your friendly banker," Gault said. "Hey, do you water ski, by any chance, Weeb?"

McDonald had a sense the right answer was no. "Never took it up," he said. "Why?"

"But you shoot skeet. And golf, right?"

McDonald nodded.

Gault shook his head. "I used to caddy... my first whiff of rich guys," he said. "I was like fourteen, humping this guy's huge motherfucker bag around. Sleazeball cheated. Kicked his ball to a better lie and had like twenty clubs in his bag. Cocksucker always gave me a dollar fifty tip. I'll never forget, four quarters, four dimes and two nickels. Every time. The richer the sonovabitch, the shittier the tipper."

Gault turned to Scaletti, who was working his first Marlboro of the day. "Del, round me up a few volunteers to ski, huh?"

Scaletti blew out a big gust of blue smoke. "Already tried, Rafe, no takers."

"Tell 'em it ain't optional," Gault said. "Get everyone out on deck. This is gonna be a great spectator sport."

Bart Brigham was in the water, holding the ski rope, his eyes darting back and forth. He raised his right arm reluctantly to Ron Jon, who was at the wheel of a twenty-two foot speed boat. Ron Jon hit the throttle and the boat surged forward. Brigham rose up out of the water on one ski. Brigham turned and looked back at the *Miss Adventure.* His eyes were suddenly filled with terror. Not more than fifty yards away, Trash Tatem and two other men stood on the suspended skeet deck, aiming shotguns at him.

Behind them, on the port side of the *Miss Adventure,* the passengers were lined up, watching reluctantly.

Frantic, Bart Brigham motioned Ron Jon to go out farther away from the boat, but Ron Jon ignored him. Brigham suddenly hunched down, trying to make himself a smaller target. Then Brigham looked back at the *Miss Adventure* and saw Gault walk up to the three men. The look on his face said it all— *this is my kind of sport!*

"Pull!" Gault shouted.

The three men fired their shotguns at Brigham and all missed.

Brigham made a series of quick turns, still down in a crouch. Gault raised his hand, then lowered it.

"Pull!"

The men fired again, and again, missed. Quickly, they reloaded as the boat pulled Brigham in closer.

"I pay you fuck-ups to be shitty shots?" Gault shouted, his face flushed with rage. "Pull!"

A blast from one of the shotguns hit the tip of Brigham's ski, but somehow he managed to stay up.

Frowning, Gault made a circular signal with his hand to Ron Jon to bring Brigham in.

"Guy deserves to live," Gault said, shaking his head. "Nice skiing, shitty shooting."

Trash Tatem, his shotgun smoking, turned to Gault. "Come on, Rafe, gimme a break. We got shotguns. Guy was outta range."

Gault just glared at him and shook his head.

Ron Jon pulled Brigham up to the swimming platform and cut the engine.

Brigham dropped the rope, swam to the platform and scrambled up onto it. Like he couldn't get out of there fast enough.

One of Gault's men walked onto the swimming platform with a flabby, unathletic-looking man in a red bathing suit. Bert Meers didn't look happy to have been chosen for waterskiing duty. Gault's man pushed Meers into the water, then tossed the ski rope to him. Meers grabbed for the rope, but couldn't reach it. Ron Jon circled around him with the boat and Meers snagged it this time.

"Come on, man," Ron Jon shouted to Meers, "you got nothing to worry about. Nothin' happened to the last guy, right? We're just puttin' on a little show for the other passengers."

Meers didn't look convinced as he waited for the rope to get taut, then raised his hand.

Ron Jon gunned it and pulled Meers up. Wobbly, Meers tried to go into a crouch like he had seen Brigham do, but almost fell over.

Gault was watching from the suspended skeet range. "Pull!" he said, all business.

His men fired and missed again. Meers went on an arc as far away from the boat as he could.

Gault walked up to Tatem and grabbed his shotgun roughly. "Gimme that fuckin' thing!"

He waved the two other guys off and they lowered their shotguns.

"Just me this time," Gault said.

Meers was fifty yards away, his legs shaking.

Gault fired once and missed. Then he reloaded and fired again.

Bulls-eye.

Meers was blown backwards as if he had just slammed into a concrete abutment. His chest was a plate-size mat of blood. He toppled over backwards as the rope skimmed along the water shooting up a white spray.

Gault looked over at Tatem.

"Out of range, huh?"

TWELVE

CLAY AND ALEXA were in her living room. Joe Dirk had his arms around a fluted column, handcuffs around his wrists.

Clay held up a knife threateningly to Dirk's neck and was holding his cell phone in his other hand.

"Hold on a second," Alexa said.

She went over and rolled up the carpet next to Clay and Dirk. Clay looked at her, puzzled.

She noticed his look and shrugged. "It's a twenty thousand-dollar dhurrie. Think I want his blood all over it?"

"Good point," Clay said, then to Dirk, "Okay, Joe, you're gonna tell your boss you followed Alexa to the bank at nine o'clock and she was in there for forty-five minutes."

Dirk nodded.

"What's Gault's number?" Clay asked.

Dirk gave it to him and Clay started to dial when his phone rang.

He didn't recognize the number.

He answered. "Hello?"

"Clay Terry?"

"Yeah, who's this?"

"My name's Anthony Nobbis, *Washington Post*."

Clay didn't respond right away. Then he started walking toward the front door. "Hold on."

He opened it and went outside.

"What can I do for you...Anthony?"

"I'm calling you from Kabul."

"That's in Afghanistan, right?"

"You know damn well where it is," Nobbis said. "I just had a very interesting conversation with one of Mohammed El Rahbi's wives."

"Which one, Judy or Barbara?"

"What?"

"Just pulling your chain, Anthony," Clay said. "I got no idea what you're talking about. Never heard of anyone named Mohammed El... whatever. And have no clue why you're calling."

"Come on, Terry, he's the guy you met for the first and last time four nights ago. Put a bullet between his eyes, matter of fact. Number three on the Isis hit list. Starting to come back to you now? Like I said, his wife positively ID'ed you as the Delta shooter."

"Is that right? So you and this guy's wife were sitting around the campfire passing the crack pipe and she just—out of the blue—came up with this crock of shit?"

"Go ahead and play your little game," Nobbis said. "Wife said no question it was you. You took out El Rahbi right after his brother."

"How'd you get this number anyway?" Clay asked.

"Let's just say I'm very enterprising."

"Listen, Anthony, you print anything about me, you got a major libel suit on your hands. Plus a bunch of enemies you really don't want to have."

"Is that a threat, Lieutenant?"

"It's Captain, asshole. And, yeah, bet your ass it is."

Clay mashed the red button and walked back into the house. "Okay, Joe, what's Gault's number again?"

Gault had just finished carving another X into the wall next to the ones for the First Officer and the two bodyguards. He handed Scaletti the knife and answered his phone.

"Yeah, Joe, what's up?"

Gault listened and a smile spread across his face. He looked over at Scaletti and gave him a fist pump. "Awesome. So she's gettin' it done." Then his expression changed. "No, no fucking way you're coming out here. I want you to stay put there. What's the matter, you don't trust me, Joey? Think I'm gonna cut you out of the deal?"

Gault listened for a few more seconds, then abruptly hung up, went over to a deck chair and sat down next to McDonald. "Your daughter was the bank's first customer this morning."

McDonald looked up at Gault and stared him down. "That man you shot, he's got two kids in high school, one in college."

"And probably a nice, fat life insurance policy."

"You're a goddamn animal, Gault," McDonald said. "You think I need convincing? Think killing people's gonna get the money here faster?"

Gault squinted his eyes, tilted his head and smiled. "Nah, that's not it at all, Weeb. What can I tell ya, my guys just needed target practice."

THIRTEEN

ALEXA AND CLAY walked down a wooden dock in the Palm Beach Marina with Joe Dirk fifteen feet ahead of them. Something was weighing heavily on Clay's mind. He stopped and turned to Alexa.

"I gotta tell you something," he said.

Alexa turned to him. "What is it?"

"You know I don't like to talk about what I do, but you need to hear this," he said, glancing down. "You might be reading about me in the papers, see me on TV."

Alexa's eyebrows arched.

"Know that Isis guy who just got killed in Afghanistan?"

"Mohammed somebody?"

"Yeah, El Rahbi," he said. "Well, I was the shooter. This reporter I just spoke to is all over the story."

Alexa nodded. "Oh, my God, Clay."

Joe Dirk turned the corner at the end of the dock. Clay raised his pistol.

"Don't go wandering off on me, Joe," he shouted. "I wouldn't mind adding to your injuries."

Dirk stopped dead in his tracks.

"Believe me," said Clay, "I'd love to have an alternative to goin' out to the boat. Like show up with six destroyers and a couple of nuclear subs, but not when a guy's got forty hostages. This way it just looks like Dirk is disobeying Gault's order, didn't want to miss his ride."

Alexa was trembling as she turned to Clay.

"Don't worry," he said, putting a hand on her shoulder. "I'll call you once I've checked into that safe room."

She threw her arms around him, holding back tears.

"This is *so* not fair," she said. "You just got here. Please, promise me you'll be careful."

Clay kissed her on the lips and pulled back. "I promise."

Alexa looked up at him and shaded her eyes. "All right then, go save our dads," she said, trying her best to smile. "We're too damn young to be orphans."

FOURTEEN

JOE DIRK WAS at the wheel of a sixteen-foot Boston Whaler, Clay in the seat behind him. Clay had on a bathing suit and no shirt. A pair of flippers, a mask, and an oxygen tank sat on the floor in front of him. A pistol, ammo clips and his cell phone, wrapped in plastic, were in his lap. He was gripping a K-bar knife in his right hand while he studied the *Miss Adventure's* floor plans next to him. His cell phone rang. He looked down at the number.

"Shit."

He unwrapped the plastic around the pistol and the cell phone. He hit the green button. "Hello."

"Terry, it's Anthony Nobbis of—"

"Yeah, yeah, the hell you want now?"

"A guy—used to be a Delta op—told me he heard from an unimpeachable source that you got a congratulatory call from Leon Panetta after you waxed El Rahbi."

Clay thought about just hanging up, then decided to answer. "First of all, who the hell is Leon Panetta?"

"You know damn well."

"And second, what does "waxed" mean?"

"Cut the shit, will ya."

"And last of all, what's this 'Delta' you keep talkin' about?"

"The Unit, the Night Stalkers. Ring a bell?"

"Never heard of 'em. Listen, man, I gotta go for a swim. It's been a real pleasure chatting with you."

He clicked off and looked off in the distance. The *Miss Adventure* was a speck on the horizon.

"So what are you gonna do with me?" Dirk asked.

"Just keep steering the boat."

A few moments later Dirk took his good hand off the wheel and—with Clay's view blocked—slipped it around a fire extinguisher mounted on the side of the boat. He was steering with the thumb and forefinger of his bad hand. He turned his head slightly and located Clay out of the corner of his eye.

He suddenly stood, whirled and swung the fire extinguisher at Clay's head like he was a batter who wanted to knock one out of the park.

Clay slid down and ducked. Dirk reared back to take another swing. In an instant, Clay hurled his knife at him. The knife twirled end over end, then slammed hard into Dirk's chest. Dirk cried out in pain and pitched forward. Blood flowed out onto the white floor of the boat.

Ten minutes later, Clay sat on the back rail, adjusted his face-mask and flipped backwards into the water.

Ron Jon, who was on lookout at the bow of the *Miss Adventure*, had seen the Whaler approaching and had gone and gotten Gault.

Gault watched it come closer, two football fields away now, and shook his head in anger. Dirk sat in the driver's seat, both hands on the wheel, heading straight for the *Miss Adventure.*

Three of Gault's men had joined him, packing Uzzis and AK- 47's.

"Told that asshole to stay with McDonald's daughter," Gault said. "The good news is she's busting her ass getting our retirement money."

Gault's men laughed, as the Whaler was half a football field away now.

"Dirk," Gault yelled, "Turn the fuck around and get your ass back to the girl's house"–then under his breath–"dumb sonovabitch."

Dirk didn't respond and his face was impassive. The Whaler was looking slightly off course now, like it was going to pass right by the *Miss Adventure* on the starboard side. It was not slowing down. Then Gault saw the blood on Dirk's shirt and the duct tape tying his hands to the wheel.

"What the…?"

Dirk suddenly keeled over and his hands tore loose from the steering wheel. The Whaler veered hard right, then slammed into the bow of the *Miss Adventure*.

FIFTEEN

CLAY SWAM UNDERNEATH THE LONG, gray hull of the *Miss Adventure*, kicking fast and smooth. In one hand was his K-Bar knife, in the other, his pistol and cell phone encased in plastic. He got to the stern of the boat, swam under the swimming platform and came up behind it. His head popped up above the ocean's surface.

The first thing he saw was one of Gault's men, standing on lookout at the fantail and another one at the stern's highest point. Holding his pistol above the water, Clay undid the plastic. Suddenly the man on the fantail spotted him and raised his Uzzi to his shoulder. But Clay lowered his Sig Sauer, aimed and fired. A bullet thudded into the man's chest.

The man two decks above heard the shot, then frantically searched the water. Finally, he saw Clay, but it was too late. Clay fired off a three-shot burst and the man toppled forward into the ocean. Clay quickly climbed onto the swimming platform, kicked off his flippers, then ran up the steps to the main aft deck. Another one of Gault's men, Rich Sanchez, heard the shots and ran down the port side cradling an AK-47.

He saw Clay duck into the master stateroom. Clay locked the door, looked around and ran toward the walk-in closet he had seen on the plans. Sanchez fired into the lock of the master stateroom, then turned the shattered doorknob and stepped inside. The stateroom looked like the penthouse suite in a five star New York hotel. Exquisite furnishings, exotic teak woods and brilliant, warm colors highlighted the bedroom. In a crouch, Sanchez swept the room with his AK-47. Then two other men, Chet Mullen and Norm Dansker, raced in.

"The hell's goin' on, Rich?" Mullen asked.

"A guy ran in here," Sanchez said, motioning to the head.

The two others inched toward it, then charged in.

Nothing.

One of them searched the closets. Nothing there either.

"Nobody here, Rich."

Sanchez eyed him coldly.

"Think I'm dreamin' this shit up? Fuckin' guy with a pistol."

Mullen raised his arms.

"Chill, man, I believe you. I'll get Rafe."

Gault and four others stood on the floor of the Whaler, huddled around the dead body of Joe Dirk. The Whaler was tied to the *Miss Adventure.*

"Somebody stuck him with a knife," Gault said, "then went over the side."

The others nodded.

Mullen, who had run up to the hull of the *Miss Adventure*, looked down at Gault and the others and waved his arms.

"Hey, Rafe, a guy with a gun. Richie saw him run into the master."

Gault nodded. Mystery solved. "Let's go get him," he said to the others.

He climbed out of the smaller boat onto the *Miss Adventure*, then ran toward the stern with the others right behind him. He turned back to Scaletti.

"What the hell's one guy think he's gonna do?"

Scaletti shrugged. "Be a dead hero."

The six men had done a search of the master stateroom but so far had come up with nothing.

"All right, take this fuckin' place apart," Gault said.

And his men did just that. They pulled down paintings, ripped up the carpet, and finally one of them pulled on a section of a bookcase, which pivoted out from the wall.

"Rafe, check this out."

Gault walked over and saw a massive solid steel door that looked like something you'd find in a bank vault.

"Well, I'll be goddamned. McDonald's got himself a panic room," he said. "Now it makes sense, the walk-in being so big on the schematic."

"What's that?" Scaletti asked.

"Nothin'."

Gault surveyed the door from top to bottom and slowly ran his hand along the outside edge. Then he rapped his knuckles on the door three times.

From the other side of the door came three knocks.

Gault shook his head and chuckled. "Got ourselves a comedian," he said, then raised his voice and spoke into the door. "Okay, pal, you're safe... for now anyway. I don't know what you're doing here, but welcome to the party."

The men surrounding Gault laughed.

A man raced through the front door, grim-faced. "Guy took out Slade and Parker. They're floatin' in the water."

Gault looked back at the steel door, then went up to it.

"You're not so welcome anymore," Gault said. "You can say good-bye to one of my hostages."

He turned to his men and smiled.

"It was time to take out another one anyway," he said. "Two of you stay here 'case this guy comes up for air."

SIXTEEN

CLAY WAS IN A FOURTEEN-BY-SIXTEEN-FOOT ROOM, with plush wall-to-wall carpeting, two big leather chairs, mahogany built-in cabinets and a closet facing a bank of recessed monitor screens. A Quotron ticker machine was flashing stock quotes on one wall, an antique slot machine sat on a stationery table next to a bolted-down foosball game. If it wasn't clear this room was designed by a man, the two-year-old Playboy calendar tacked to a wall confirmed it.

At eye level were four rectangular steel hatch doors. Clay dialed his cell phone and Alexa answered breathlessly.

"Thank God, you're okay," she said.

"I'm fine. Helluva man cave Webb's got here," he said, looking around. "Case of Heineken, two fifths of Meyers Rum, Cuban cigars, whole buncha frozen foods, even a couple quarts of Ben & Jerry's. Beats the hell out of Army MRE's."

"What's that?"

"Dog food they feed us."

"And there's no way they can get in?"

"No way. This place is a steel and Kevlar fortress. Couldn't drive a tank through these walls. And the best part is my new wardrobe. I got some of it strapped on now. A tactical body armor vest. This ballistic neck and shoulder protector, a bulletproof helmet and face guard."

"No clue what any of that is."

"I'm like Superman, bullets bounce off me. Plus I got sharp shooter's rifles, flash bangs—"

"Jesus, Clay, you sound like a kid in a candy store. Just promise you'll be careful with your new toys."

"Don't worry. Hey, I didn't mention, there are two less bad guys than before. Actually three, counting Dirk."

"Good riddance," said Alexa.

"Anyway, I gotta go to work, time for me to do a little exploring."

Gault and Scaletti walked up to McDonald. "Forgot to mention you had a panic room?" Gault said.

"You never asked."

"Who's in there?" asked Gault.

"What do you mean?"

"Some guy got on board, killed three of my men. Who the hell is he?"

McDonald threw up his arms. "Jodie Foster? How the hell would I know?"

"What?"

"I got no clue. You been listening in on all my calls."

"Guy got here by boat," Gault said. "Whoever he is, he's safe for now, but you ain't."

Gault handed McDonald a cell phone. "I wanna talk to your daughter. Call her."

McDonald dialed the cell, then handed it to Gault.

Alexa, sitting at her laptop, pushed the button on her cell. "Hello?"

"Who's the guy you sent out here?"

"Excuse me?"

"Cut the shit, who is he?"

"I have no idea what you're talking about."

"Fine, play it that way. Guy's dead meat anyway," Gault said. "How you comin' with my money?"

"I need at least an extra day."

"No can do."

"Will you take half then?"

"Ask again and I double it," Gault said, hammering the red button on the cell.

Shaking his head and glowering, he looked over at McDonald. "Bitch is stalling me."

"No, she's not. She's—"

"Bullshit. She's stalling and negotiating and some poor fucker's gonna pay for it."

He gave Scaletti, standing next to him, a head flick. They walked away from McDonald. "Go get four of McDonald's guys. Tell 'em to strap on their Speedos and meet me poolside."

A sinister look spread across Gault's face. "I'm gonna find Tatem and his little metal box. Time to have some fun."

SEVENTEEN

CHARLIE HARROW, Bart Brigham, and two other men, Tom Voss and Jack James, were standing at the deep end of the swimming pool in bathing suits. They had the frightened looks of four men in a concentration camp.

Gault was standing on the diving board, a whistle in his mouth, Scaletti off to the right of the other men.

"Okay, boys, let's see how fast you are," Gault said. "Take your positions."

The four men just looked around at each other.

"Come on, you heard the man. Take your positions," Scaletti shouted.

The men walked to the edge of the pool and crouched down in racing dive positions.

"Okay, boys, so listen up. I'm calling it the *Race of your Life*. Three winners and one loser," Gault said. "And trust me—you *really* don't want to be the loser."

He clapped his hands together like a gung-ho swim coach.

"Okay, up and back three times," he said, raising an arm. "And no rules. So use your imaginations and have fun. On your mark, get set..." He waited a torturous few seconds before blowing his whistle. "Go!"

The men dove into the pool.

Gault looked over at Scaletti and smiled. "Better swim like you got alligators up your asses."

Scaletti laughed.

Leading the others, James did a flip turn at the end of the pool.

The other three, a little behind him, just touched and turned.

Trash Tatem walked in with his metal box that had the holes on top. He stepped up to the edge of the pool as the men were on the second half of their first lap.

James and Voss were a half-length ahead of the other two. As James was about to pass the next lane over, Brigham slammed him in the face with his elbow.

James, dazed and bleeding, slowed to a dog paddle. Voss and Harrow made the second turn, and as they did, James grabbed the leg of Voss, who was slightly ahead of him. James pulled Voss back, grabbed him around the shoulder, then threw an arm around his neck and started choking him.

Gault clapped enthusiastically. "That's what I'm talkin' about."

On the side of the pool, Trash Tatem twisted off a round metal section at the top of the box. Cautiously, he peeked in. In a lightning motion, he reached in and pulled out a thick, writhing black snake. It was a cottonmouth. Casually almost, he flipped it in the pool.

Gault gave Tatem a big thumbs up of approval. The snake started swimming in the direction of James, who was still choking Voss.

Harrow on his final lap, looked over and, in horror, spotted the snake. His arms churning faster, he touched the wall, pulled himself up, and swung both legs up over the side of the pool. The look on his face showed he was infinitely relieved to be out of the water.

Brigham was laboring as he turned for home. Then he looked up, spotted the snake and stopped dead. Hesitating momentarily, he went under water and, hugging the bottom of the pool, swam his final lap under water, below the snake. Reaching the end, he scrambled out of the pool even faster than Harrow had.

Voss, who had broken free from James, touched and turned toward his final lap, not having seen the cottonmouth. Swimming like a man possessed to beat James, he was on a collision course heading straight for the snake.

Harrow and Brigham looked on in horror. Brigham yelled a warning.

As Voss approached, the snake raised its head up out of the water and struck him in the face. Voss screamed and stopped a foot from the snake. He looked up and saw it. Before he could react, it struck him again, hitting him in the eye this time. Voss screamed again, but this time it was far more bloodcurdling, a combination of terror and pain.

Hearing the scream, Jack James watched as Voss swam, desperately, to the end of the pool. Somehow Voss pulled himself up and out of the pool.

"Help! Help! Please!" Voss cried out.

Harrow rushed over to him, but there wasn't much he could do.

The snake slithered toward James. James, his eyes bulging with fear, swam to the nearest wall, planted his arms on the coping and vaulted up out of the pool. He had had enough.

Scaletti walked over to him. James was breathing in short gasps and eyeing the snake.

Scaletti started shaking his head. "Sorry, man, but you didn't finish," he said. "Not sure you're gonna like what you get for last place."

EIGHTEEN

CLAY SAT in a big leather chair in the safe room. He put down a sheet of plans that had been spread out in his lap. Then he got up and went over to a rectangular steel hatch on the far wall and opened it. He looked into a tight, narrow tunnel. He could see that it was built within the *Miss Adventure's* existing air conditioning duct system and looked to be approximately two feet high by three feet wide. Directly below it was the hatch to another tunnel, and to its right were two more, above and below each other. Each was barely large enough for him to crawl through. He couldn't help but think McDonald would get stuck.

Clay pulled himself up like he was doing a chin-up and climbed into one of the dark tunnels. He snaked his way through it, feeling extremely claustrophobic. At the other end, he opened a hatch door and saw that he had come out directly under a sleek, powerful-looking, teal green helicopter. It loomed above him, protectively almost. He noted that the tunnel provided a great escape. If only all the hostages and crew could fit into the helicopter.

He crawled backwards and dropped down out of that tunnel back into the safe room.

Then he pulled himself up and crawled into a second tunnel. He wormed his way through it to the end. Then slowly he opened the hatch. It went to a small room with low ceilings. It resembled a small, poor man's version of the safe room, with minimal furniture and decorations. He crawled back, dropped down to the floor, then hoisted himself up into the third tunnel.

It was the longest one so far and had a downward incline. At the end of it, he was looking directly into a head, off of what looked to be the crew's quarters. He watched as a man entered, then, painstakingly, combed his ratty, long blond hair. Then a few minutes later another man came in. It reminded him of looking into an aquarium, watching the fish swim by.

The man's face was no more than a foot away from Clay's. From the man's perspective, he was simply looking into a mirror. But from Clay's, it was a two-way mirror. After a few seconds, Clay backed up and went back down the tunnel into the safe room. He knew he had just faced two of Gault's men at point-blank range.

A few seconds later, he climbed up into the fourth and final tunnel which ended up behind a fully stocked bar. Clay heard voices on the other side of the bar and, fearful of getting spotted, disappeared back into the tunnel.

Gault and Scaletti were leaning on the railing, looking off into the distance.

"We gotta get that bastard," Gault said.

Scaletti nodded and spat over the side as Gault's phone rang. He looked down at it and smiled. "Hey, bud."

He listened, then pumped his fist. "Atta boy, I knew you had it in ya. Okay, first thing we're gonna do at your new home is goin' out and hooking a big 'ol swordfish."

He listened, as a grin spread across his face. "Love you too, now go hit the books."

He clicked off and turned to Scaletti. "Where were we? Oh, yeah. Go get my brother, will ya? Make it seem like you just picked him at random. Slap him around a little if you have to."

Scaletti nodded and walked back to the aft salon.

A few minutes later he was back with Dave Gault. They were in a section of the boat where no one could see them. Dave was holding his jaw. "Mother fucking dago slugged me," Dave said to his brother.

"Sorry, man, wouldn't want the crew thinking you might be on our team," Scaletti said.

Dave shook his head, grimaced and looked at his brother. "So what's up?"

"I need you to get me some information," Gault said.

"What do you wanna know?"

"Specs on the safe room," Gault said. "See what your buddy the captain knows. Or the engineer maybe."

"Okay. I'll see what I can find out," Dave said. "That it?"

Gault nodded.

In a flash, Dave reared back and slammed Scaletti in the chin with his fist. "Sorry, man, didn't want my crew mates thinking I'm a pussy."

McDonald and Harrow were talking in hushed tones, sitting in a couch in the aft section.

Ten feet away, one of Gault's men, Lou Horak—red-bearded and barrel-chested—stood guard.

"I would have figured Alexa to be going out with some investment banker type," Harrow said.

"Yeah, well, then you don't know Alexa."

Harrow nodded his approval. "Delta's got Saddam Hussein and Zawahiri. Seals just got better PR."

"How's that?"

"Obama... joined at the hip with the Seals after they got Bin Laden. Figured it'd get him votes."

"Spoken like a true Republican."

Harrow laughed and stood up, stretching his legs.

"Delta's are the best. They quietly get it done. Seals, they kiss and tell. Remember that one, on the Seal team that took out Bin Laden, who wrote the tell all?"

McDonald nodded. “I remember,” he said. “Clay actually started out as a Ranger.”

“I figured. That’s where they get most of ‘em from,” Harrow said. “But they only take like one in fifty of the Rangers who apply.”

Gault was back in the fantail, when Scalleti came up to him.

“Dinner’s up in a half hour, Rafe,” Scaletti said with an evil smirk. “This is gonna be good.”

Gault smiled back. “Gotta check out something on the schematics now,” he said, “but I wouldn’t miss it for the world.”

The galley on the *Miss Adventure* was eat-off-the-floor clean and spotless and looked like a Zagat five-star kitchen from a New York restaurant. The chef and his sous-chef were looking stressed and tense as they put silver serving platters containing filet mignon, artichoke hearts and risotto on the dumbwaiter.

Two of Gault’s men were lurking in the background, automatic weapons at the ready.

Clay was in the safe room, watching a monitor, when he saw Gault walk out onto the main deck. He picked up his pistol and crawled up into the tunnel, which led to the crew’s quarters.

He looked at his watch when he got to the two-way mirror at the crew’s head. It was 6:15. He just waited, hoping Gault would poke his head in. He looked at his watch a little while later. It was 6:38.

Not this time.

He crawled back into the tunnel, dropped down into the safe room, then went back to the monitor. He saw Gault, plate on his lap, eating dinner next to Scaletti. Gault swung around when he heard the whir of the dumb waiter. He caught Scaletti’s eye and smiled.

The dumbwaiter opened slowly and Cassandra, standing in front of it, suddenly dropped her plate and screamed. Diane, next to her, started shrieking hysterically. Everyone turned to the dumbwaiter in horror. On a large silver platter was the severed head of McDonald's friend, Jack James—the swimmer who came in last. In his mouth was a shiny red apple.

Scaletti took the last bite of his steak, then looked up at Gault. "Don't forget the X."

NINETEEN

CLAY HEARD the screams through a microphone. It was so loud it seemed like the women were in the safe room with him. Leaning closer to a monitor, he saw the decapitated head.

He didn't move for a few moments, then dialed Alexa.

"I want you to promise me something," he said.

"What?"

"That you'll never bring the money out here yourself."

"Why? What happened?"

"Nothing, just don't do it, okay?"

"What if Gault says that's the only way he'll let anyone go?"

"I don't care. Then he'll have you, your father and the money. And no reason to let anyone go. I gotta go, Lex."

Clay eyed his phone. His battery life was down to twenty percent.

Enraged, he crawled through the tunnel to the head and faced the two-way mirror again.

His watch said 7:10. He was like a hunter up on a stand, waiting for a deer to enter his kill zone. The only sounds were his deep breathing and his ticking watch. He tapped the glass wall impatiently, bit his lip, and looked down at his watch. 7:36.

He waited for another half an hour.

Then he crawled back through the tunnel.

Once again, mission not accomplished.

He dropped back down onto the floor of the safe room. Suddenly, a voice came from one of the hidden mikes. It was a voice he hadn't heard in a long time.

"Whoever's in there, this is the captain. I hope you can hear me."

Clay hurried over to one of the monitors. His father's hand was covering his mouth. He was talking into one of the unseen microphones buried in a wall.

"I want to help if I can," said his father. "I don't know what you've already figured out, but me and my crew are in the fantail salon on the port side. Webb and the others on starboard. There are four tunnels —" Then he paused. "Gotta go."

Clay watched the man with the ratty blond hair approach his father. His face got to within six inches of Curt Terry's. He just eyed Curt malevolently for a few seconds, then sneered and walked away.

Clay stood up and put on a bulletproof vest, then the neck and shoulder protector, and finally, the ballistic helmet and face-mask. He walked toward the door with his pistol. He racked his gun, put his ear to the door, and hunched down in a crouched position.

He slid back the massive bolt, then shoved the door open. Two men were watching TV on the far corner of the room.

Clay quickly took dead aim at one, who tried to bolt out of his chair. But Clay squeezed off one shot, which slammed into his chest. The other man was on his feet, his Mac 10 spitting bullets. One hit Clay in the chest protector. He fired off a burst and the man crashed backwards into a wall and crumpled to the floor. Clay heard footsteps thudding toward him and ran over to the man and tore the Mac 10 out of his arms. Then he sprinted back into the safe room as a flurry of bullets slammed into the walls and door behind him.

On the monitor he saw Gault and Scaletti run in—a few seconds too late. Gault looked down at his two men, lying on the floor.

"I want this fucking guy and I want him in a thousand little pieces!"

A few minutes later McDonald, playing backgammon with Harrow as Jess looked on, overheard a conversation between two of Gault's men about the shoot-out that had just taken place in his bedroom. And about Gault's two men who had been killed. McDonald got up, went over to the wall where Gault had carved the four crude X's and, with a letter opener from a nearby desk, carved two X's on another wall a few feet away.

Gault walked in just as he was finishing. "What the fuck are you doing?"

"You're keeping score and I'm keeping score," said McDonald.

Gault walked up to him and slapped him with the back of his hand, sending him reeling backward.

"Do that again and you're a dead man," Gault said. "Now who the hell's in there? Nobody risks their ass like that unless they're blood or your daughter's payin' 'em a fuckin' fortune."

"Only one my daughter's payin' a fortune to is you," McDonald said, holding his jaw.

Gault eyed him like he wasn't buying it. "What's her number again?"

McDonald told him and Gault dialed on his cell.

"Hello," Alexa said.

"Game's changed, doll," Gault said. "I need you to get me the money tomorrow."

He listened, then went ballistic. "I don't want to fuckin' hear it. No money, no Daddy. Get it here by two tomorrow."

He clicked off and looked like he wanted to hurl his cell phone at the wall. Then he sighed, shook his head and stormed off.

Harrow watched him go then looked up at McDonald. "I been thinking," he said. "Once he gets the money, we're all dead."

McDonald nodded and rolled the dice. "I know, I've been thinkin' the same thing."

Jess leaned toward the men. "I might have an idea."

Alexa got out of her car and walked into a one-story brick building surrounded by palm trees. It had a discreet sign that read, "Drug Enforcement Agency, Miami, Florida."

Ten minutes later, she was sitting in an office across from a handsome man in his early thirties who filled out his suit nicely.

"And here I thought it was 'cause you missed me. Realized what a terrible mistake you made," said the man.

"Very funny, Jake," Alexa said. "We're thinking about building a hotel in the Keys, but not if drug guys are shooting it out on the streets every day. Seems like you guys let it turn into the Wild West down there."

Jake frowned, got up, and walked over to his door. He glanced down the hall, then closed it.

"Just what the hell are you talking about, Lex?"

"I'll tell you exactly," she said. "'*Four Executed, Drug Lord Suspected'* The Miami Herald, May eighth. '*Dealer Slain, Rival Questioned,*' Sun-Sentinel, June tenth. Want me to go on? The name Rafe Gault keeps coming up."

Jake shook his head and smiled confidently. "Oh, him. You don't need to worry about him anymore."

"Really? Why's that?"

Jake tapped his desk with his fingers. "This isn't exactly something I'm s'posed to talk to civilians about."

"Is that all I am to you, Jake, a civilian?" Alexa said with a pout. "Promise I'll be discreet."

Jake nodded. "Okay. We got that guy Gault on the run. Man's gone completely quiet."

"Is that a fact?

"Yeah, absolutely," Jake said. "We put so much heat on the dude, he's moving out of the country."

TWENTY

HORAK AND DANSKER, on guard duty, were leaning up against the bar.

Jess and flirty Diane, dressed to kill and showing a lot of skin, came out of the ladies' room across from the guards. The two strutted over to the guards.

"You guys mind if we get a drink?" Jess said, with a seductive smile. "Hard day at the office."

Horak and Dansker traded looks. They both shrugged. "Yeah, sure, why not?"

As they started toward the bar, Diane turned back to them. "Why don't you boys join us? We hate drinking alone."

Jess winked. "Or won't that nasty Mr. Gault let you?"

A half hour later all four did yet another round of tequila shots. A Patron bottle—nearly kicked—sat in front of them.

Flirty Diane had her arm around the waist of Dansker.

Jess and Horak were behind the bar. His eyes, a little glassy, were locked onto Jess's ample cleavage. She fluttered her long lashes.

"How 'bout you and me slip off to the master stateroom?" Horak whispered, in his crude interpretation of sexy.

"But aren't you...on duty?"

Horak flicked his head at Dansker. "He can handle it."

Jess sized up Dansker as he and Diane knocked back their umpteenth shot.

Jess grabbed Horak's hand and led him off.

In the stateroom, Horak peeled off his shirt and pants and got down to his skivvies faster than Speedy Gonzalez.

He looked over at Jess. All she'd taken off were her shoes. "Come on, girl, whatcha waiting for?"

Jess flashed her bedroom eyes and sashayed over to him.

She put her arms around Horak as her eyes darted around, looking for his gun. She finally spotted it on a bureau behind him.

Horak leaned forward to kiss her as she reached around him for the gun. She picked it up and pressed it into the back of his head. "Love scene's over, Romeo."

Suddenly Gault barged in, a gun trained on Diane's head. Behind him, Scaletti had a gun up to McDonald's cheek and Ron Jon had one aimed at Harrow.

"Put it down, girlfriend," Gault said.

Jess didn't move.

Gault gestured to Diane. "Want me to blow her pretty little head off? 'Cause you can be damn sure I will."

Jess lowered the gun, then put it on the floor. Horak backhanded her hard. "Bitch!"

Gault let Diane go, walked up to Horak and whacked him with the butt of his gun. "Stupid fuck. Brain in your goddamn dick as usual!"

Harrow, still in Ron Jon's grip, stepped forward and held up his hands. "The whole thing was my idea."

Gault turned to Harrow. "Was it now? Well, shame on you, Senator. You gonna have to pay for that."

He tossed a pair of handcuffs at Scaletti, then turned to the women with a big smile.

"And you two, a friend of mine's got big plans for you."

TWENTY-ONE

ALEXA WAS PACING in her living room, a cocktail in hand. She dialed her cell and waited as it rang.

Clay was in his leather chair absorbed in a page of the boat's schematics. He didn't answer right away, then he clicked on. "Hey, babe."

"Oh, thank God," Alexa said. "Every time I call I wonder if you're going to answer or—"

"You worry too much."

"How can I not?" Alexa said. "So I got intel on Gault."

"You Google him or something?"

"Give me a little more credit," Alexa said. "Old boyfriends come in handy sometimes."

"What?"

"Jake Parsons. Head of the DEA in Miami, remember?"

Clay frowned. "Yeah, I remember."

"They've been trying to nail Gault for years. Apparently, he just sold his house in Islamorada. The movers showed up yesterday."

"Keep going."

"Jake told me all Gault's stuff is going to a place called Baja Bolivar, an island off of Columbia. A guy—Ernesto somebody—put a deposit down on a house there for him."

"So that's where he's going after the big score."

"Yup, and fun fact number two. Gault was an Army Ranger."

"*You gotta be kidding.*"

"Nope," said Alexa. "Highly decorated. Highly deadly."

"Last part sure is true," Clay said.

"Third thing is, I'm up to $120 million. Any chance he'll take that, you think?"

"You know how it is... the guy wants $300 million, I want a Lamborghini. So maybe I end up with a Mustang and he gets a measly hundred twenty mill. But meantime, I'm gonna do whatever I can so he ends up with nada."

"I know you are," Alexa said. "How you doing there anyway, in your little man cave?"

"Well, I may have found a way to get the psychopath."

"How?"

"Okay, so clearly your ol' man thought of everything," Clay said. "There're four tunnels from the safe room. One leads to a head in the crew quarters. Used to be the crew quarters anyway, 'til Gault and his men commandeered it."

"I know all about the tunnels," Alexa said. "I helped design 'em."

Clay chuckled. "Why am I not surprised?"

"The one you're talking about was built so the crew could escape to the safe room if intruders came on board. Gault doesn't know it's there, right?"

"No reason he would. It just looks like a mirror," Clay said. "Gotta hand it to you, it's a hell of a good escape route. Crew members smash the window, crawl in and go to the safe room. But what's that other little room?"

"That was actually Dad's idea," Alexa said. "It's the back-up to the safe room. In case the safe room ever got breached."

"Which is highly unlikely," Clay said.

"But not impossible."

"Okay, so ten minutes ago, I was staring eyeball to eyeball with one of Gault's guys admiring himself in that mirror."

"Bet it crossed your mind to change his expression."

"Yeah, it did, but I figured I only get one shot."

"And you want to use it on Gault."

"Exactly."

"Gotcha."

"Only problem is," Clay said, "I have no idea whether that's the head Gault uses."

Alexa paused for a second. "Yeah, 'cause a guy like him… probably just whizzes over the side."

TWENTY-TWO

GAULT'S MEN were herding McDonald and his friends into the vast master head, which was easily the size of a racquetball court. Everyone clustered around the three glass walls of a huge ornate shower that looked big enough for a whole football team to shower in at once.

Gault led a handcuffed Charlie Harrow up to the door, then turned around and addressed the small crowd like a ring announcer at a boxing match.

"In keeping with my policy of wanting to provide you with plenty of quality entertainment, I want to welcome you this afternoon to my very own version of the Ultimate Cage Match." He unlocked Harrow's handcuffs and looked up. "Anyone remember Russell Crowe taking on the tiger in *Gladiator*? Or, my personal favorite, The Rock, going up against the king of the jungle in *Hercules*? Well, tonight, we've got an even more exciting match-up. In one corner…" Gault shoved Harrow, all scrawny five foot five of him, through the door, then continued in his best Michael Buffer voice. "*All the way from Tallahassee, Florida…* Senator Stone Cold Char-lie 'The Ex-e-cu-tion-eeeer' Harrow!"

Gault's men snickered at the sight of Harrow, who looked more like a meek little mouse than a Stone Cold anything.

Trash Tatem with his long metal box came up behind Gault.

"And in the other corner..." Gault turned to Tatem. "From way out west in the Sonoran desert... I give you Harold the—"

He glanced over at Scaletti. "Horrendous."

"Harold the Horrendous… Gila monster!"

The woman spectators gasped as Tatem reached in, grabbed the two-foot long Gila Monster and tossed it into the shower.

It looked savagely menacing as its long brown tongue darted in and out.

Ron Jon, MAC-10 in hand, turned to McDonald. "I got fifty bucks on Harold," he said. "Give you three to one odds."

McDonald nodded. *Game on, motherfucker.*

Harrow, eyes wide with fear, stepped back a step as the Gila monster crawled toward him pinning him up against a wall.

It looked ready to strike just as Harrow jumped to his left.

"Quick move by the Senator," Gault announced, "just in the nick of time!"

The Gila lunged at Harrow again.

Harrow took three steps to his right as the Gila monster followed. Sweat dripped from Harrow's brow as, slowly, the Gila backed him into a corner.

Harrow's eyes, desperate, flashed around. He turned to the glass wall, jumped up, grabbed the top and pulled himself up, just inches out of the Gila's reach.

As if milking the suspense, the Gila scrabbled up to the wall right under Harrow, waiting for him to drop.

Harrow's arms were quaking. He looked like he couldn't hold on much longer.

All of a sudden, Gault's men started chanting as if they were the chorus in the *Gladiator*'s amphitheater. "*Kill! Kill! Kill! Kill! Kill!*"

Ron Jon turned to McDonald. "Ten to one on another fifty?"

McDonald nodded again.

Harrow reached one hand over the other and repeated it. He was slowly working his way along the wall, putting a little distance between himself and the Gila.

"Come on, Charlie, hang in there!" McDonald yelled.

"You can do it!" Jess exhorted.

Harrow's whole body was trembling now, as if he were operating a jackhammer.

With all he had left, Harrow shoved off from the top and landed, shakily, ten feet away from the Gila monster.

The Gila turned and glared at him.

Harrow dropped down into a crouch and took off a shoe.

Gault raised an eyebrow, entertained by the spectacle.

Harrow lobbed the shoe over the Gila. It landed with a thud behind it. Instinctively, the Gila's head reared back and struck at the shoe.

Harrow seized the opportunity and stepped forward, grabbing its tail. Then he lifted it up and smashed it hard into the glass wall. He took it back and whipped it into the wall even harder.

McDonald started to chant. "*Kill! Kill! Kill!*"

Then his friends joined in. "*Kill! Kill! Kill! Kill! Kill! Kill!*"

Blood was spurting from the Gila's mouth and spattered the glass wall, but Harrow was still not done.

Viciously, he slammed it against the wall three more times, then panting, he tossed it into a corner. It wasn't moving.

Harrow, spent, crumpled to the floor.

McDonald cheered loudly and thrust his hand out to Ron Jon for his money.

Tatem, enraged, stepped into the shower and aimed his gun at Harrow.

But Gault waved him off. "Forget it, Trash. You gonna have to go back to the desert, find another Harold."

TWENTY-THREE

GAULT, up at the bow of the *Miss Adventure* where no one could hear him, was talking into his cell phone, just above a whisper. He looked around to make sure no one was near.

"Ernesto, change in plan. I want you to pick me up tomorrow."

He listened for a few moments.

"No, it's just gonna be me and my brother."

He listened again, then laughed. "No sorry, your amigo Mr. Scaletti will not be joining us."

It was just starting to get dark. Ron Jon was standing next to the red Ferrari tender, perched above the main deck, looking down at Snow.

"The hell you doing up there, Ronny?" Snow asked.

Ron Jon smiled. "I figured out a way to smoke out the dude in the safe room."

"You run it by Rafe?" Snow asked.

"Nah, Rafe likes it when we get creative," Ron Jon said. "You know, show a little initiative."

Snow looked dubious. "Oh, yeah? Since when?"

Ron Jon ignored Snow's skepticism and went over to the controls of the hydraulic lift, fumbled around with them for a while, but finally figured out how to lower the Ferrari down from its perch to the deck below. Once it was down on the aft deck, Ron Jon unhooked the cables around it, opened its front door, and hopped in.

He turned on the ignition, smiled at Snow, and revved the powerful engine for a few seconds.

"Hey, do me a favor," Ron Jon said to Snow. "Open the doors to the fantail and make sure everybody's off to one side. Don't want to run anyone down."

Snow shrugged. "Okay," he said, "you sure you know what you're doin'?"

Ron Jon shot Snow a scornful look. Snow walked over to the fantail twenty feet away, opened the doors and ushered a few passengers off to the side.

Ron Jon gave him a wave, revved the engine once more, threw the gearshift into forward and floored it. Tires squealing, the car was a fire engine-red blur as it blew through the open French doors of the fantail salon and hurtled toward a wall. The crew and hostages watched in stunned amazement. Then suddenly the driver's side door opened and Ron Jon rolled out like a wannabe stunt driver.

The Ferrari slammed into the wall doing a shade over sixty.

Ron Jon, lying on his side on the deck, slowly flexed his right arm and touched his bloody nose gingerly. Then he shook his head in disappointment at the sight of the crumpled, smoking but miraculously still running Ferrari thirty feet away. It had not crashed through the wall as he had expected. He pounded the fist of his good hand on the deck. "Shit," he yelled.

Hearing the explosion from the bow of the *Miss Adventure*, Gault ran back to where Ron Jon was getting to his feet.

Gault raised his arms and gave Ron Jon a withering stare. "What the hell you think you're doin'?"

Ron Jon forced a smile. "Tried to crash through the wall. I know how much you wanna get the guy in there."

Gault put his hands on his hips and shook his head. "You forgot who's calling the shots here?" Then, under his breath, "Fucking cretin."

Ron Jon slinked away, holding his arm.

He went past Snow, who looked amused. "Guess I'll keep my creativity to myself," Snow said under his breath.

Coming across the deck, Scaletti, shaking his head, walked up to Gault.

"What the hell was that about?" Scaletti asked.

"Un-fucking-believable," Gault said. "He decided to ram the Ferrari into the safe room."

Scaletti shrugged. "Tryin' to impress the boss, huh."

Gault looked over at the smoking Ferrari. "Stupid fuck oughta stick to killing people. He's good at that. Gave me an idea, though."

The chopper was thumping loudly one hundred feet above the *Miss Adventure*. Bart Brigham, a bandage on the side of his face from the violent swim race and looking like a scared rabbit, was piloting. Gault had gone to Curt Terry and asked him who could fly the helicopter. The captain, trying to protect his men, said no one on his crew could fly it. Then Gault had asked the passengers. Two of the girls had eyeballed Bart Brigham.

Gault and Scaletti were sitting behind Brigham. Gault had the Stinger on his shoulder and was aiming it at the roof of the safe room below.

"Don't miss, man," Scaletti said.

"You just worry about taking out the hero," said Gault, then to Brigham. "Get a little closer."

Brigham lowered the helicopter a few feet.

Gault pulled the trigger and the missile blasted into the roof of the safe room below.

There was a fiery explosion, then smoke mushroomed out in all directions.

The impact left a gaping ten-foot hole in the roof.

In the breached safe room below, Clay, decked out in armor, looked up at them, aimed his pistol, and fired. A bullet crashed into the chopper's fuselage.

Scaletti fired off a long burst, as Clay ran toward a tunnel and practically dove in. He dropped down through the tunnel and hit the floor below with a heavy thud. He was in the room half the size of the safe room, which Webb McDonald had designed as a back-up to the safe room, should the safe room ever get breached. It had a low ceiling, which his head almost touched. Unlike the safe room, it had just one monitor. Overall, a definite downgrade.

The main safe room, which Clay had just vacated, was smoldering. It had a big, jagged hole in its roof. Gault had ordered Bart Brigham to land the helicopter and now he and Scaletti, automatic rifles in hand, were surveying the demolished safe room. They looked up and studied the four tunnels.

Gault pointed at one. "See where it goes, Del."

Scaletti shook his head. "No way, man. I ain't crawlin' down no badger hole. Not with the badger in one."

Gault scowled, knowing there was no way he was going to talk him into it.

"Hey, how 'bout we roll a bunch of grenades down 'em," Scaletti suggested.

Gault thought for a second, then shook his head. "Bad idea. We got no idea where these things go. Could end up sinking the whole goddamn ship."

Gault looked around, went over to a shelf, and grabbed a bottle of rum. He opened a hatch to one of the tunnels and smashed the bottle on the inside, breaking it. "Oughta slow the guy down a little," Gault said, looking at the jagged glass shards.

Scaletti followed his lead and went and got another bottle. He smashed it on the inside of a second tunnel. Then they did the same with the other two. Gault looked around the safe room. "Like we got a game of Wack-a-Mole here," he said. "Get someone up here, Del, to smoke him if he crawls out."

TWENTY-FOUR

GAULT AND SCALETTI were back at their positions: smoking a cigar and a cigarette, leaning up against the starboard rail, gazing out over the ocean.

Gault was taking a leak over the side. "I got a theory where our guy is."

"Where?"

"I checked out the floor plan schematic," Gault said. "The ship was built with a sauna connected to the master. My guess is McDonald retrofitted it into a back-up safe room."

"Guy was a little paranoid, huh?" Scaletti said with a chuckle. "About bad guys coming on board."

"Yeah, terrible to be so suspicious," Gault said with a smile. "The sauna is right above the galley."

"You thinkin' about getting at it from the galley?"

"Yeah, maybe the walls aren't as thick as the primary safe room. It's worth a shot," Gault said. "Hey, I spoke to your buddy Ernesto again. He's payin' me the seventy-five mil for this sucker. Turns out he's actually got a deep-water dock off that island he owns. By the way, half the seventy-five million is in blow."

Scaletti shook his head admiringly.

"And if I know you, you already got the blow sold off on the street. Probably at a hundred percent markup."

"Yeah, most of it's already spoken for."

"I love it, man. You got it comin' and going. I mean, shit, the chick bringing out three hundred mil, 'nother seventy five for the yacht, the coke…"

Gault smiled and took a long drag on his cigar.

"Christ, man," said Scaletti, "fuck McDonald. You're the all-American success story, not him."

Gault lowered his head and did his impression of humble. "I 'preciate your vote of confidence, Del."

Scaletti laughed and slapped him on the shoulder. "Hey, I figure the more for you, the more for me," he said. "So the Columbian's pickin' us up on his sub?"

"Yeah, after he makes a drop in the islands."

Gault's phone rang. He looked down at the number and punched his cell.

"Hey, honey. How's the move goin'?"

"It's me, Dad," the boy's voice said. "You coming home soon? I miss you."

"Hey, bud, I miss you, too," said Gault. "I'm gonna meet you and your mom at our new home. I can't wait to see you there."

"Me, too, Dad," the boy said. "Catch a lotta fish out there?"

"Oh, yeah, " Gault said. "One really big one. See ya soon, pal."

Gault clicked off and smiled at Scaletti.

"Oh, and not to mention," Scaletti said, "world's greatest Dad."

Clay's wrist-watch alarm went off, but he was already wide awake. He looked down at it. It was 12:30 AM. He listened, heard the sounds of snoring coming from one of the bugs and looked at the monitor of the aft salon.

Just about everyone was asleep. He dialed his cell. He noticed that his battery life was down to ten percent.

Alexa answered on the first ring. "You okay, honey?"

Her stress level sounded like it had amped up a notch.

"Yeah, I'm fine. I'm in a new place now."

"Where's that?"

"The back-up safe room."

"Thank God Dad thought of that."

"I know, but if the safe room was the Ritz, this is a Motel 6," Clay said. "I gotta go, I'm running low on juice. Left my charger in the safe room. I just wanted to check in."

"What's your next move?"

He looked up at one of the tunnels. "I'm lonely in here," he said. "I'm gonna go find me some roommates."

Clay screwed a silencer into his pistol. He stood, opened a hatch, and pulled himself up into the tunnel. He crawled through it to the end, then slowly opened the hatch. His head was about a foot away from a row of liquor bottles. He crawled out, got into a crouch, then raised himself up and peeked up over the bar.

It was the spacious aft room in the fantail section, which Clay remembered from the time he visited his father on the boat. He saw bodies sleeping in chairs, couches, on the floor, all around the room. Some looked comfortable, most didn't. Lights from the ship's deck partially illuminated the room. His eyes adjusted and slowly swept the room. On the starboard side, he saw Webb McDonald sitting on the floor, his back against a wall, asleep. Two of Gault's men, one with a shaved head and the other with a red beard, bracketed him on either side. The eyes of the man with the red beard flickered shut, then a few moments later, opened up again. The man with the shaved head was wide-awake smoking a cigarette and cradling a machine gun.

Clay's eyes shifted to his left. He saw the crewmen in rumpled uniforms, most of them asleep on the floor, several sprawled out in chairs. One was awake, though, standing. It was his father. Clay's eyes stayed on Curt Terry for a few seconds, but Terry didn't look over. Clay got into a crouch again, went around the end of the bar, and got down on all fours. He started inching his way across the floor, his pistol in his right hand while keeping an eye on the two guards.

Then he accidentally bumped into a sleeping woman.

Her eyes snapped open with fear.

Clay put his hand over her mouth and whispered softly, "I'm one of the good guys."

She nodded, but didn't seem sure who he was. He took his hand off her mouth, went flat on the floor, and got down in a crawl. He was twenty feet from MacDonald and his guards now. The man with the shaved head took a drag on his cigarette then looked up and, seeing movement, raised his Uzzi. Clay aimed his Sig Sauer and squeezed off one shot from the silenced pistol. The man emitted a guttural groan and pitched forward.

The red-bearded man, suddenly wide-awake, jerked up his automatic. Again, Clay took just one shot. The guard crashed backwards through a picture window. Suddenly the room was chaos. Clay ran to McDonald, lifted him up and shoved him in the direction of the bar.

"Take some of the women and go," Clay said.

McDonald grabbed Ali's and Cassandra's arms. "Come on," he said.

The three sprinted toward the bar. As they rounded the corner of it, Ali slipped and twisted her ankle. She cried out and went down hard. Cassandra tripped over her and fell on top. McDonald turned and came back to them, but Ali signaled to him. "I'm fine," she said. "You go. We'll be right behind you."

McDonald started to help her, but she shooed him off.

Bart Brigham and another man, Bill Dunne, watched McDonald and the women making their escape and ran after them. They raced around the end of the bar, then shoved the women out of their way and scurried into the tunnel.

Meanwhile Clay had run over to his father. There was a small but unmistakable smile of pride as Curt realized it was his son in the safe room. Curt pointed to his ankles, which were handcuffed together. "Get out of here!" Curt signaled frantically. "Go!"

Clay's eyes locked onto his father's and held there for a split second. Then he turned and charged toward the bar. As he got near it, he put his hands out, grabbed the edge of the bar and hurtled up over it. Just as he hit the floor on the other side, bullets slammed into the bar and the wall above him.

Ali and Cassandra were still struggling to get into the tunnel. Clay lifted the injured Ali up and pushed her in, then did the same for Cassandra. Then he stood, looked up over the bar, and fired at Trash Tatem and another man who had just raced into the room.

Clay ducked back down behind the bar as a volley of gunfire from the two men sprayed the wall above him. Clay turned, crouched down, then hurried into the tunnel. He pulled the hatch to yank it shut, but something was blocking it. He saw the butt of a gun and kicked at it, but couldn't move it. He kicked at it again, but it still wouldn't budge.

He turned and scrambled down the short length of tunnel and felt someone's hands grab his and pull him into the back-up safe room. He landed hard on the floor and looked up at Webb McDonald.

McDonald slammed the hatch door behind him as a bullet clanged off it.

"Jesus, you all right, Clay?" McDonald said, helping him up.

Clay looked around at the three men and two women and nodded. "Hey, Mr. McDonald, yeah, I'm fine."

"You can lose the Mr. McDonald. Just call me Webb."

"Okay... *Webb*," Clay said, looking around. "Rest of you okay?"

Ali was not okay. In a rage, she turned to Brigham and Dunne. "You call yourself men? Knocking us out of the way and crawling over us?"

Brigham just smiled his smarmy smile and tried to shrug it off. "Sorry, honey, sometimes it's just every man for himself."

McDonald stared at him coldly and shook his head. "Are you kidding? That's pathetic."

"Don't lecture me, Webb," Brigham said. "I don't want to hear it."

McDonald turned to Clay. "You tried to get Curt, huh?"

"Yeah, but his legs were shackled."

"I know."

Clay eyed McDonald's hair, then smiled. "New 'hairdo', Webb?"

McDonald chuckled. "Compliments of the guy you're gonna kill."

"Sure you don't want to do the honors?"

"Only thing I ever shot were quail," McDonald said.

"Men are much bigger targets."

Clay dialed his cell and hit speaker. He noticed his battery life was down to four percent.

"Got someone who wants to say hello," Clay said when Alexa answered.

He handed McDonald the phone.

"Hey, sweetie," said McDonald.

"Oh, thank God, you're okay," Alexa said.

"God had nothing to do with it. Thank Clay," McDonald said.

"And you're in the back-up room now?" Alexa asked.

"Yes, wish we'd made it a little bigger," McDonald said.

There was a click on Alexa's phone. Call waiting.

Alexa looked down at the number.

"Hold on, that's Gault," she said.

Alexa pressed the button.

"Hello?"

"Your old man's in with the hero, thinking he's safe and sound," Gault said. "We'll just see about that. In any case, like I said, tomorrow at two or I torch this sucker. If you're not here, they either fry or drown."

TWENTY-FIVE

THE WALL CLOCK in the safe room said 1:15 in the morning.

Clay and McDonald were crouched down, talking. Brigham, Dunne, and the girls were sitting on the floor listening.

"By my count, there's six left," Clay said to McDonald. "That jibe with yours?"

McDonald thought for a second, then nodded. "Yeah, I'm pretty sure that's right."

"He's got a manpower problem, Gault does. Between covering the hostages, posting guys in the safe room, and now that tunnel, they're spread thin," Clay said. "Our job is to spread 'em even thinner."

McDonald nodded. "Whenever you're ready."

Gault was shining a flashlight into the tunnel behind the bar. Scaletti poked the barrel of his M-203 grenade launcher into it. Gault studied the near hatch.

"Damn thing's four inches thick," Gault said. "I doubt a grenade's gonna blow open the other end."

"Let's give it a shot anyway," Scaletti said. "This sucker's pretty powerful."

Gault shrugged, nodded and stepped away.

Scaletti pulled the trigger on the M-203.

There was a jarring, deafening explosion as the projectile slammed into the hatch a few feet away from Clay and the others in the safe room.

Ali threw her hands up to her ears and screamed even louder than when she saw Jack James's severed head.

"Jesus Christ!" McDonald said. "What the hell?"

Clay examined the hatch. Surprisingly, it looked intact. "Sounded like a grenade-launcher," he said with a smile. "Pretty solid ship you got here, Webb."

McDonald smiled and patted a wall. "Damn straight."

Shaking his head, Gault looked into the tunnel behind the bar.

"I told you. Damn things's built like Fort Knox," he said, then with a diabolical grin. "Gave me another idea, though."

Clay suddenly smelled something and started sniffing. He eyed McDonald. He could tell by the look on McDonald's face, he smelled it too.

"Carbon monoxide," Clay said, moving closer to the hatch.

McDonald glanced at the monitor. "Look at this," he said, pointing to the monitor.

Clay leaned over and looked. On it, he saw exhaust fumes rising from the smashed Ferrari. The car was laboring noisily but running nevertheless.

"Shit," Clay said, seeing a hose from the Ferrari's exhaust leading into the tunnel behind the bar.

McDonald coughed as Clay examined the hatch.

"There's a hairline crack in it," Clay said.

As the smell spread throughout the small room, Brigham turned to Clay, panicked. "Well, shit, man, fix it!"

Clay stared at Brigham. "Aye, aye, sir, I'm on it," he said sarcastically, then turning to McDonald. "Got any electrical tape in here?"

McDonald opened a drawer and looked around. "How 'bout this?"

He pulled out a Costco-sized box of Juicy Fruit gum and handed it to Clay.

Clay smiled, nodded, ripped it open and handed a pack to Brigham. "Start chewing."

Scaletti coughed and waved his hand. The carbon monoxide had reversed direction, going back down the tunnel toward Gault and Scaletti.

Gault shook his head, furious. "Bastard plugged the hole somehow," he said.

He climbed into the Ferrari and killed the sputtering engine. Then in a rage, he slammed the door hard, almost knocking it off its hinges. His cell rang. He stabbed at the green button. "This better be good, Dave."

He listened, started nodding, then did something resembling a double take. "Holy shit!" Gault said.

"What?" Scaletti asked.

"Dave says the guy in there's from the Unit."

"You mean...same outfit you were in?"

"No, man, I was a Ranger. Rangers are elite, but Delta's...Delta's are fuckin' killing machines," Gault said. "I oughta know. I almost was one."

"Almost?"

"Yeah, my CO told me I didn't have enough respect for authority."

"What did you say?"

"Told him to go fuck himself."

Scaletti laughed. “So what’s the guy doing out here?”

Gault glared at him like it was the dumbest question he had ever heard.

“Oh, I dunno, Del, killin’ our guys for one thing?”

“No, I mean—”

“I know what you mean. All I know is Dave overheard the captain talking to another guy,” Gault said. “Found out something else, too.”

“What’s that?”

“We got a bunch of C-4 aboard,” Gault said, referring to the powerful plastic explosive.

“You’re kiddin’?” Scaletti said. “Why would McDonald have C-4?”

“Fuck if I know. Fourth of July maybe?” Gault said. “Or maybe ’cause billionaires can have whatever the hell they want.”

TWENTY-SIX

CLAY WAS TALKING TO MCDONALD. It was three thirty in the morning. Everyone was hyper; no one could sleep.

Clay pointed up at the tunnels. "Where do the other two tunnels go?" he asked. "Only had a chance to go down the two on the left."

"Let's see...they tie into the same ones that come off the safe room," McDonald said, pointing. "That one goes to the crew's head. That one comes out under the chopper."

Brigham perked up. "Hang on, Webb, you got a tunnel to the chopper?"

McDonald nodded.

"Well, Jesus, what are we waiting for?" Brigham asked.

McDonald eyed him like he was a six-foot cockroach. "You think I'm going to leave my friends and crew behind?"

"Hey, that's your call, but no reason Bill and I can't go, take the girls with us," Brigham said.

Ali shook her head vigorously. "I'm not going anywhere with you."

Cassandra nodded her agreement.

"Fine," Brigham said. "But I got no interest in hanging around here waiting for these mutts to figure out how to kill us."

Bill Dunne nodded his agreement.

"You crank that thing up, they'll be firing on you in five seconds," Clay said.

"Five seconds is all I need," Brigham said, "It goes two hundred miles an hour."

"Trust me, it's not worth the risk," Clay said.

"And sittin' around in this rathole *is*?" Brigham said with a sneer.

TWENTY-SEVEN

GAULT AND SCALETTI were in a large room with gleaming stainless steel, industrial-size kitchen equipment surrounding them. It was three forty-five in the morning and they were there with Abel Crow, the ship's engineer, a bald man in his sixties who was sweating profusely. He was balanced on a stepladder, taping a clay-like explosive to the ceiling. It was C-4.

Scaletti had his gun on Crow as Gault read something on his laptop.

"How many pounds you got there?" Gault asked.

"About four."

Gault was reading an article on the internet. "Add two more," he said.

The engineer looked around at him, alarmed. "That might be too much."

"Chill, pops," Gault said, "so maybe the boys and girls get nicked up a little."

McDonald, Ali, Cassandra, and Dunne were asleep in the safe room. Clay, who hadn't slept more than a few hours in the last seventy-two hours, was nodding on and off. His eyes flickered, then shut. Brigham, wide-awake, watched Clay's eyes close. Then he elbowed Dunne. Dunne's eyes opened. Brigham put his forefinger up to his mouth, shushing him, then pointed to Clay, then the tunnel.

Moments later a hatch opened on the top deck of the *Miss Adventure*. Brigham, looking wired, poked his head out. He and Dunne crawled out of the tunnel and slid into the seats of the formidable-looking helicopter.

Brigham, in the pilot's seat, turned the ignition, shifted the stick forward, and the AW149 went straight up like a rocket.

Tatem and Scaletti ran out of the galley and fired up in the air. The helicopter continued to accelerate.

Then Gault appeared, a big grin on his face. Strapping the Stinger onto his shoulder, Gault shook his head at Trash Tatem. "Let me guess, out of range again, Trash?"

He looked up, aimed and waited for the distinct click of the Stinger "locking" onto the heat of the helicopter engine's exhaust.

Click.

Gault squeezed the trigger. There was a thumping sound and a phffffft as the missile blasted out of the Stinger tube. A second later, there was a shattering explosion and a huge, fiery light show illuminated the starless sky.

Gault blew triumphantly on the smoky butt end of the missile launcher, eyed Tatem and chuckled. The blazing helicopter seemed suspended in air for a split second, then started falling, picking up speed fast. The three men watched, mesmerized, as it tumbled and fell. Suddenly they realized it was headed straight for the *Miss Adventure.*

In the safe room, Clay heard the noise of the chopper's powerful engine and bolted upright. Then came a huge explosion. McDonald and the two women were wide-awake now, listening in horror.

Gault, Scaletti and Tatem watched the trajectory of the falling fireball and ran into the fantail. Through the skylight, they watched the fiery helicopter crash into the roof of the captain's bridge. The boat shook like it was struck by an earthquake tremor and in seconds the bridge was a blazing inferno. But the *Miss Adventure*'s powerful fire extinguishing system kicked on automatically. Water and halon started spraying and extinguishing the fire.

"Jesus Christ, Rafe, fifty feet to the right and it would have landed on our goddamn heads!" said Scaletti.

"Why do you think I waited that extra second?" said Gault.

Scaletti gave him a searching look, but Gault had on his best poker face.

McDonald shook his head and looked over at Clay.

"Poor bastards."

Ali looked up at McDonald. "Poor boat."

A half hour later the girls were sleeping while McDonald and Clay talked.

"He wasn't exactly a 'friend,'" McDonald said about Brigham. "More like a guy who had a certain knack for sniffing out where the party was. I'm just glad he didn't have a wife, wasn't a father."

Clay nodded.

"Speaking of fathers—"

Clay shook his head. "Let's not."

"You don't think I know the whole story?" McDonald said. "I've spent a hundred days a year on this thing with Curt for the past twenty years."

Clay just sighed. It was not enough to slow McDonald down.

"How he's pissed at you for going to Afghanistan when your mother got sick, and you're pissed at him for the same damn thing. 'Cept he was out here." McDonald paused. "Sad part is your mom's gone, but since you two are still around, it's time you made up? Buried the hatchet?"

Clay mulled it over but didn't respond.

"And while I'm on my soapbox, when are you going to make Alexa an honest woman?"

Clay chuckled. "I always hated that expression."

"Well?"

Clay sighed and locked on to McDonald's eyes. "Okay, Webb, wanna know the truth?"

"Damn right I do."

"'Cause I'm scared shitless of coming home."

"Why?"

"'Cause I'm really good at what I do over there," Clay said. "I'm not really sure what I'd do here. Plus, as you know, unemployment among vets is way above the average."

"Jesus Christ, Clay," McDonald said, shaking his head. "I'd hire you in a heartbeat."

Clay smiled. "Thanks, Webb, but no offense, head of security for McDonald International is not what I had in mind."

"I'm not talk—"

"Another thing: us Delta's got a pretty shitty record in the marital department."

McDonald thought for a second. "Know what, Clay," he said finally, "sounds like you're using a bunch of statistics to talk you out of shit. If I thought like that when I was young and broke, I'd be sitting around with my thumb up my ass—*old and broke*."

TWENTY-EIGHT

7:05 A.M., three hours later.

McDonald and the two women were sleeping, jammed together on the floor.

Clay, one hand on his stubbly chin, was gazing off into space, thinking how he didn't have much time left. He looked at his watch, got up, stepped over Ali, then looked into one of the tunnels. He reached up to the one leading to the crew's head and hoisted himself into it.

He crawled down the tunnel until he was, once again, facing the back of the mirror in the head. He just watched and waited, his gun pressed up against the glass. He looked down at his watch. It was 7:28. Then he heard a voice in the distance.

"Hey, Rafe. Time to rise and shine, man. It's Wednesday. Payday." He recognized the voice as Del Scaletti, Rafe Gault's right-hand man.

Clay heard a muffled response and recognized it as Gault's voice, though he couldn't make out the words. He tightened his grip on his gun.

Scaletti entered the bathroom, rubbing his eyes. He looked into the mirror, turned on the faucet, then doused his face with water. He looked into the mirror again. The jagged scar on his neck looked like someone had slashed his throat with a broken beer bottle. His teeth were nicotine stained and his gums bulbous. Clay aimed his gun at a spot right between his eyes, but didn't pull the trigger.

Scaletti turned and walked out of the head.

In the distance, Clay saw Gault walk past the door to the head. He aimed his gun, but Gault was gone. Then he crossed back again, almost like he was pacing. Clay figured he could hit him, but maybe not kill him. He wanted to have a sure kill shot. He waited for Gault to come into the bathroom.

But he never did.

A half an hour later, Gault and Scaletti were on the deck of the *Miss Adventure.* Gault looked restless and edgy. Gault dialed his phone and brought it up to his ear.

"Got a present for me, doll?" he asked when Alexa answered.

"I'll be at the bank when it opens to make the withdrawal," she said. "I'm going to get a man who works for my father to drop it off. I'll just tell him—"

"Whoa, whoa, whoa... You're not gonna tell him nothin'. 'Cause you're bringing it out to me in person. Period. End of story," Gault said. "Get here by two with all of it"—Gault flipped his Zippo—"or I torch this motherfucker."

TWENTY-NINE

ALEXA, looking agitated, was standing in a lavish office on the other side of an expensive mahogany desk from a man with horn-rimmed glasses and a grey flannel suit.

"What do you mean, we're five million short?" Alexa said, putting her hands on her hips.

"I'm sorry, Miss McDonald," the banker said. "But as I told you on the phone, we need more collateral to give you the rest."

"My family's been banking here for three decades and you can't bend your requirements just an inch?" Alexa demanded.

"We already have," said the banker. "I'm sorry but this is the best we can do."

Alexa took a deep breath, turned, and hurried out the door.

Curt Terry, shackled, had his hand over his mouth, so his captors couldn't tell he was talking into the hidden mike.

"Hope you guys can hear me," Curt said in a loud whisper. "Just so you know, Webb, they found that C-4. I don't have any idea what they plan to do with it, but my guess would be to get at you somehow. If I find out, I'll try to let you know. And Clay, as that crusty old bastard George Patton used to say, time to quit screwin' around and blow the rest of these redneck motherfuckers to hell and gone."

Ron Jon, Mac-10 in hand, suddenly came up behind Curt. Curt didn't hear him coming.

"Talkin' to yourself, Cap?" said Ron Jon.

Ron Jon looked around suspiciously, then spotted the bug planted in the wall. He turned quickly and swung his rifle butt at Curt, smashing him in the jaw. Curt's head snapped back and blood streamed from his nose and mouth. Ron Jon whirled with his gun again and slammed Curt in the stomach.

Curt went down, his head hitting the deck. Ron Jon kicked him repeatedly in the ribs, then once to his head, a sick smile plastered on his face.

Snow walked up to Ron Jon. "Dude, you gonna kill the guy?"

Ron Jon looked at Snow and smirked. "Got a problem with that?"

Snow thought for a second and scratched his bristly chin. "No, not really."

Ron Jon laughed, then booted Curt in the ribs one last time.

Clay, an expression of barely contained rage, glared at the monitor helplessly as Ron Jon kicked his father again, Rodney King-style.

Clay looked away from the monitor, then snapped a clip of ammo into his Sig Sauer. He looked around the small room and breathed deeply a half dozen times. McDonald walked over to Clay and patted him on the shoulder.

"We'll get the bastard, Clay, don't worry."

Clay nodded slowly and deliberately, then looked back at the monitor.

Charlie Harrow, Jess, and Dave Gault were helping Curt get up. Harrow was wiping blood off his face as Dave Gault was standing by with a bandage in his hand. Jess handed Curt a bottle of water.

"You okay, Captain?" Dave Gault asked.

Curt grimaced and did his best to nod.

Rafe Gault walked up to the microphone that Ron Jon had discovered.

Clay and McDonald were glued to the monitor as Gault approached it.

"I'd like to welcome aboard the member of the prestigious Unit," Gault pointed to the hidden camera. "Guess you guys been watching the show for a while. Well, allow me to introduce myself properly. I'm a retired sergeant, Third Ranger Battalion. Four deployments, recipient of Meritorious Unit Commendation, Purple Heart, honorably discharged after I got hit during Operation Anaconda, Takur Gur."

He inched closer to the monitor, his face flush against it, a cluster of white hairs in his beard.

"I got twenty-nine confirmed kills." Gault smiled broadly. "I'm lookin' to make it an even thirty."

THIRTY

ALEXA RACED up to her house, jammed on the brake and ran inside.

Sweat running down her cheek, she unloaded a drawer full of expensive-looking jewelry into a Hefty garbage bag.

Then she ran down to a sideboard in her dining room, opened a large mahogany box, pulled out vintage silver knives, forks and spoons, and put them into the garbage bag.

Teetering on a chair, she took down a painting from the wall, then rolled up the expensive dhurrie rug.

Clay turned to McDonald. Both were fitted out with armor and protective gear. "Guy's got a pretty impressive resume," Clay said.

McDonald slapped him on the shoulder. "I'll take yours any day."

"Sure you're up for this?" Clay asked.

"Absolutely," said McDonald.

Clay smiled, then he and McDonald stepped over the two sleeping women and climbed into the tunnel that went up to the safe room.

Clay was inching his way along when his hand came down on something sharp.

"Shit!" he said, feeling sudden pain.

"What's wrong?" asked McDonald, right behind him.

Clay reached above carefully and felt another shard of glass. "Look out, there's broken glass all over."

Inching along gingerly, Clay got to the end of the tunnel and could see clear blue sky. From the end of the tunnel, he scanned the safe room. No one was there. He crawled out into the safe room, which had big chunks of concrete and dust all over the floor, and looked down at his bloody hand. He rubbed it on his pants.

McDonald came up right behind him.

Clay turned and walked toward the door leading to the master stateroom.

He turned back to McDonald. "Ready?"

McDonald nodded and smiled gamely. Clay could see both fear and anticipation.

Clay gestured McDonald to stay low. Then he counted off with his fingers...*one...two... three!*

Clay thrust his shoulder into the door and they charged through it, firing, before they'd even spotted their targets.

Clay saw a man jump behind a couch in the sitting room part of the stateroom and blindly squeezed off a few shots.

Then he dove to the floor and fired another three rounds into the couch. He heard a low moan and the thud of a body fall to the floor on the other side.

Clay looked over at McDonald who was flat on the floor, aiming his gun in the direction of the stateroom's head. Amped up with adrenaline, McDonald pointed frantically at the head. "In there," he said under his breath.

From his vantage point, Clay could see Snow's reflection in a bathroom mirror. Snow moved a few steps toward the door, his gun raised.

"He's all yours," Clay whispered, and pointed, "six inches right of the switch plate."

Without hesitation, McDonald fired a long burst into the spot Clay had just described.

Snow staggered backwards, then toppled into a massive Jacuzzi.

Clay gave McDonald a thumbs-up. "Nice shootin'," he said. "Man's takin' himself a nice, long blood bath."

They suddenly heard feet pounding on the deck and got up and ran back into the safe room. Clay gave McDonald a boost up into the tunnel, then followed him in. A few moments later, McDonald hit the floor of the back-up safe room, Clay right behind him.

The girls slept right through it.

Clay closed the hatch and pulled off his helmet. "Nice job. Just cut the pirate population by one third."

McDonald smiled and nodded. Shooting guys seemed to agree with him. He looked around, picked up a kitchen knife, and carved two X's into the wall.

"What are you doin'?" Clay asked.

McDonald looked back at him. "Just a little something I learned from Gault. Two down, four to go."

Gault, Scaletti and Tatem stared down at the dead men. Then Gault looked up. On his face was the steely gaze of a soldier intent on revenge.

"Time to jam the C-4 up that Delta's ass," he said.

THIRTY-ONE

CLAY WENT over to the tunnel next to the one they'd just come through. He reached up, grabbed the sides and looked over at McDonald. "I gotta hit the head."

McDonald smiled and nodded.

Ali woke up, rubbed her eyes, and looked down at the still sleeping Cassandra.

Turning to McDonald, she said: "I miss anything?"

"Nah, been pretty quiet around here," McDonald said with a straight face.

Clay was in a familiar position. Lying in wait. Looking through the back of the two-way mirror into the crew's head. Then, from a distance, he heard a door open. Then footsteps. Ron Jon entered the head. He took a leak, then stepped up to the sink and mirror, but didn't wash his hands. Instead he just looked at himself. Stroked his chin. Smiled. Turned his head and looked sideways into the mirror, seemingly smitten by what he saw. Clay tapped his raised pistol softly on the two-way mirror. Ron John heard it and froze.

Then, there was an ear-splitting explosion. The shattering of glass. Then a long echo.

Ron Jon had a massive hole between his eyes.

Clay lowered his Sig Sauer. "I would have preferred your boss, but you'll do."

He backed down the tunnel and dropped down into the safe room. He smiled at McDonald, went over, picked up the kitchen knife and carved an X next to the ones McDonald had just carved. McDonald smiled at him and slapped him on the back. "Gault?" he asked expectantly.

"No, that mutt who beat up my old man."

"Almost as good."

Clay nodded.

Her hair mussed, face shiny and armpits stained, Alexa was driving like a bat out of hell. Her car had stuff piled to the roof in the back. Paintings were stacked in the front seat. The dhurrie rug stuck out a back window. Trash bags were everywhere, even a high def TV was jammed in the back.

She glanced at the clock on the dashboard—11:32 a.m.

Her phone rang. She jumped. "Stressed out" didn't begin to describe it.

On the phone was Satan.

"Got my money, doll?" Gault asked.

"I'll be there by two."

Gault, standing next to Abel Crow in a corner of the galley, clicked off his phone and gave Scaletti the thumbs-up.

Crow was getting ready to detonate the C-4 with a blasting cap. Gault signaled to Scaletti and Tatem to take positions in different areas of the kitchen. The three got their guns ready and crouched down.

"Okay, Pop, let 'er rip!" Gault yelled to Crow.

Crow hesitated.

"Hit it!"

The engineer hit the detonating cap. Another massive, violent, shattering explosion reverberated throughout the boat, even louder than when the helicopter crashed into the Captain's bridge. Smoke and dust billowed out everywhere.

Three shots rang out, then a pause, then several more. Out of the smoke and dust, a man's figure appeared.

The air cleared... it was Clay, down on one knee, firing his pistol. He looked around for McDonald and the women. But they were nowhere in sight. He stood up and sprinted through a nearby doorway.

"Scaletti?" Gault yelled through the dust and smoke.

"Yeah?" Scaletti said, coughing.

"Where the hell are they?" Gault shouted.

"I don't know."

"Tatem?" Gault cried out.

Nothing.

Then the smoke cleared. Tatem was lying in a heap, blood pooling on the gleaming white floor next to his chest. Gault shook his head, ran over to the gaping hole in the ceiling and looked up. Scaletti followed and they both aimed their guns up at the safe room. But nobody was there.

"I couldn't see shit after it went off," Gault said, then motioned to Scaletti. "Come on!"

The faces of the hostages back on the fantail were shrouded with fear. They had heard the series of gunshots, then just minutes ago, the huge explosion, then more gunfire.

Gault charged into the fantail, yanked Jess out of her chair, and held her in front of him. Scaletti did the same with Brett. Then Gault, his eyes black with rage, shouted, "Okay, Delta, I'm gonna blow this bitch's head off and turn this place into Columbine 'less you get your ass out here. *Now!*"

Charlie Harrow was watching twenty feet away. He was holding McDonald's wafer thin remote control card in his hand. Harrow heard the whir of the dumbwaiter and glanced over at it. Inside the dumbwaiter, Clay was peeking out. Scaletti, hearing it, looked over and spotted Clay. Scaletti jerked his pistol up and started firing, using the girl as a shield. "Rafe, the dumbwaiter!" he yelled.

Gault swung around, spotted Clay and fired off a burst.

Bullets clanged off the dumbwaiter as Clay ducked down. He couldn't shoot back for fear of hitting one of the women shields. Outgunned and trapped, Clay just squatted down as low as he could. In his eyes, primal fear.

Harrow searched the thin card, then pressed a corner of it. Suddenly, a craps table from the casino came whirring up out of the floor. Clay jumped out of the dumbwaiter, tucked and rolled on the floor, then dove into the ascending craps table. Bullets thudded into the thick wooden side of it but did not go through. It was a perfect four-sided fortress. He peeked up over one side and saw that he had a sliver of a shot at Scaletti.

He fired off three quick shots. One of them slammed into Scaletti's right shoulder. Scaletti's grip around Brett's neck loosened and she dove for safety. Wincing in pain, Scaletti dropped his gun. Gault, his left arm tight around Jess's neck, started backing up out of the room.

Inside the craps table, Clay raised his gun but had no shot at Gault.

Gault backpedaled with Jess shielding him. He backed up to the stern of the boat, went down the steps to the swimming platform, and holding Jess in a tight chokehold, got into one of the go-fast boats.

Gault started the engine and looked up and saw Clay come around the port side of the stern. Clay had his own shield now: his arm was around the neck of Scaletti, who was wounded and bloody. Gault aimed his gun at Clay.

"Tit"—Gault gestured at Jess—"for tat"—then gestured at Scaletti.

Gault raised his gun.

"Jesus, Rafe, don't shoot," Scaletti yelled.

Gault was reversing slowly in the go-fast boat. "You're so damn skinny, Del," Gault said, "bullet probably'd go right through you."

A look of panic gripped Scaletti's face.

"Sorry, Del, you were gonna miss the boat anyway."

"No, Rafe, Jesus—"

Three bullets ripped into Scaletti's chest.

THIRTY-TWO

THE BULLETS DID NOT GO through Scaletti, but they did kill him.

Clay watched Gault jam the go-fast boat's accelerator forward and roar off. Clay dropped the lifeless Scaletti, ran down to the swim platform, and aimed his pistol at Gault. But Jess still shielded Gault, who was putting distance between them by the second. Clay checked the other boat's ignition and saw the key in it. He jumped in, started it up and gunned it.

Jess suddenly reached up and grabbed Gault's hand, which was around her neck, and with both her hands, tore it off her. Then she ran to the rear of the boat. It looked like she was thinking about jumping into the water when Gault suddenly cut the throttle. The boat slowed and Jess tumbled back to where Gault was standing, one hand on the wheel. He grabbed her roughly by the arm and jammed the throttle forward again.

Clay's boat had made up some distance. They were about a football field apart now.

Clay saw Gault swing around and look back at him. Gault aimed and fired his Uzzi at Clay. Clay ducked down as two bullets ripped into his bow.

Jess suddenly bit down hard on Gault's wrist. He took his hand off the wheel, grabbed her by the hair and slapped her hard. She fell to the deck. With Gault no longer steering the boat, it started weaving wildly from side to side. He hauled Jess up and grabbed the wheel again. But Jess—with nothing to lose—was not done. She took a desperate swing and knocked Gault's Uzzi out of his hand into the ocean.

Gault backhanded her in the face, then looked up to see Clay in his boat twenty feet away. Clay had Gault dead in his sights. An easy kill shot. He started to squeeze the trigger as Gault's unblinking eyes bored into his.

Then Clay lowered his Sig and jammed it into his waistband.

He cut the wheel to his left and got side-by-side with Gault's boat. Then he jumped over the side of his boat, grabbing the gunwale of Gault's boat. Gault spun his wheel left, then right, trying to shake Clay off into the ocean. But Clay pulled himself up and over the side. Then he got into a crouch and charged Gault. He got off a blistering left to Gault's jaw. Gault crashed back against the side of the boat. The boat, with no one at the wheel, was weaving wildly. His balance shaky, Clay lunged at Gault and unleashed a roundhouse right. But Gault blocked the blow. Then Clay lowered his head and slammed Gault with a head butt.

Gault was reeling and Clay slugged him in the side of his face. Gault staggered backwards, his legs rubbery. Gault's arms were rotating as he tried to regain his balance. But he couldn't and he toppled over the side of the boat into the ocean.

Clay crabbed over to the driver's seat, grabbed the wheel and did a U-turn with the boat. He looked down at Jess. "Are you all right?"

She nodded, but looked like she might be in shock.

Clay put one hand over his eyes and scanned the ocean up ahead. He didn't see Gault right away. But then, twenty yards ahead, he spotted him. Gault was dog paddling weakly, like he was about to go under.

Clay speeded up and looked around inside the boat. He spotted a gaffers hook in a pile with other tools. Maybe used for snagging marijuana bales out of the ocean, he guessed. He glided up beside Gault, reached down with the hook, and spiked it into the back of his shirt.

He pulled up, but it ripped through Gault's shirt. He angled it back down, hooking it onto Gault's belt. He pulled him up over the side with the hook and his other hand and let him drop to the floor of the boat.

Then he cut the boats engine, looked around, saw a rope and tied him up.

Breathing in short gasps, Gault looked up at him, taking a few moments to focus.

"Professional courtesy back there," Clay said. "Couldn't put one between the eyes of any Ranger. Not even you."

"You might live to regret that," Gault muttered.

Five minutes later, they approached the stern of the *Miss Adventure*. As they pulled up to the swimming platform, Clay saw another boat tied to it and recognized it. There were five large green duffel bags in it. He tied up the Donzi and helped Jess out.

"Sure you're okay?" he asked her.

"Yeah, now I am," she said. "Now that you got that bastard."

"You did a hell of a job out there."

He looked down at Gault, prone on the bottom of the boat, bleeding from his nose and mouth. Their eyes met, Gault smiled. "It ain't over 'til it's over, Delta boy."

Clay just shook his head. "It's over."

He heard footsteps, turned, and saw Alexa running toward him. She ran down the steps to the swimming platform.

"Oh thank God," she said, throwing a huge hug around him.

She looked up at his face, noticing his cuts and bruises, then touched him gently on the cheek. "You don't look so good, honey."

Clay flicked his eyes at Gault whose head was turned away from them and seemed unconscious. "As they say, you should see the other guy."

He kissed her, then glanced up and saw his father approaching.

They locked eyes for a second but didn't say a word. Then slowly, Clay walked toward his father. They were ten feet apart.

"I don't know about you," Curt said, "but I'm not real big on man hugs."

Clay laughed, took a few more steps, grabbed his father around the shoulders, pulled him close, and bear hugged him. "Get over yourself, Pop."

Curt laughed and hugged his son back. Like he was going to squeeze the air out of him. Alexa was smiling, watching their long-awaited reunion.

"Isn't that sweet," she said.

Curt and Clay were still hugging. "I never really took you two for huggers," Alexa said.

They were still hugging.

"Okay, boys, break it up," Alexa said. "Time for my own heart-warming reunion with *my* own father."

A crew member, Fred Parmenter, walked down to the swimming platform and came up to Curt.

"Anything I can do, Cap?"

Curt pointed to Gault, who seemed to be unconscious now, on the floor of the go-fast boat. "Take him to the pilot house. Watch him like a hawk."

Clay put his arm around Alexa's shoulder, then his father's. They walked up the steps to the boat, heading toward the galley.

When they got there the smell of C-4 was stifling, the dust and smoke in the air, oppressive.

All three looked up at what was left. It looked like a close-up of Hiroshima.

"Where is he?" Alexa asked, looking at Clay.

"I'm not sure."

They were all looking up when suddenly McDonald's dirty, bruised face appeared. He was one story above them, standing on the edge of what had once been the back-up safe room.

"Hi, guys," McDonald said, cracking a wide smile.

Alexa's face lit up. "Oh, Daddy, there you are."

"You all right, Webb?" Curt asked.

"I'm okay, but my ears are still ringing. Not used to these damn explosions every five minutes," McDonald said, looking around. "My poor boat sure took a beating."

"It can all be fixed," Alexa said. "You, on the other hand, could not have been."

"What happened to the girls, Webb?" Clay asked.

Two frightened but relieved faces peered out from above on either side of McDonald.

"I'm here," said Ali.

Cassandra waved her fingers. "Me, too."

"We're on this little ledge up here," McDonald said. "About all that didn't get blown to hell."

"We'll get you a ladder," Curt said, looking around.

A few minutes later, McDonald climbed down a ladder. He turned and embraced Alexa. Covered with dust, he had an ear-to-ear grin. The women just looked happy to be alive and in one piece.

Then Alexa looked up at McDonald and burst out laughing.

"You got a new barber, Daddy?"

McDonald smoothed down his Mohawk and smiled.

"I'm getting kinda used to it. Think it'll fly in Palm Beach?"

"Sure. If Webb McDonald has one, everybody's gonna want one," Alexa said.

THIRTY-THREE

CLAY, Alexa, Curt, and McDonald walked back out onto the deck.

"I'm gonna check on the crew," McDonald said. "Come on, Curt."

Curt nodded as Fred Parmenter approached.

"I put in a call to Coast Guard District Seven. Apprised them of our situation," Parmenter said to Curt. "Should be here in an hour, they told me. Gault's in the pilothouse. We got a man on him."

Alexa's eyes narrowed. "I want to have a few words with that sonovabitch. Come on, Clay."

Uzzi slung over his shoulder, Clay walked across the deck to the pilothouse with Alexa.

Gault's face was bloody, but his sneering arrogance was still there. He was handcuffed and being guarded by a member of the crew who had a Glock pointed at his head.

Alexa walked up to Gault and stared at his bloody face. "So you're the guy who likes blood so much."

She reared back and slapped him hard. He didn't see it coming, but smiled back at her.

"And you're the bitch with my money," he said.

"Yeah, too bad you'll never get to spend it."

Out of nowhere, the crewman kicked the Uzzi out of Clay's hands, took two steps forward, and grabbed Alexa around the neck.

It was Dave Gault.

He shoved the Glock up against Alexa's cheek roughly. Then he turned to Clay. "Okay, hero, on the floor, face down."

Clay hesitated but stayed on his feet.

Rafe Gault stepped forward.

"Nice goin'," Gault said to his brother, gesturing to his tied-up hands. "Untie me."

With one hand, Dave deftly untied the rope. Then Gault picked up Clay's Uzzi from the floor, and with his other hand, backhanded Alexa hard across the face. "Back atcha, bitch."

Clay took a step toward Gault, but Dave and Gault turned their weapons on him.

"I'm sick of this goddamn boat," Gault said to his brother. "We're gonna take hers and the cash, then tell Ernesto to pick us up somewhere else."

Dave nodded and pulled a knife out of his waistband and put it up to Alexa's neck. At the same time, Gault aimed the Uzzi up to Clay's head, just above his ear. Clay was silent, just eyeballing Gault.

"Start beggin', motherfucker, or you're number thirty."

Clay stared at him, unblinking.

Gault smiled and pulled the Uzzi back.

"Okay, guess I owe you one. We'll let blondie go when we're done with her. Might be a while, 'cause it looks like she could be a lotta fun."

In a quick motion, Gault slammed the butt of the Uzzi over Clay's head.

Clay fell to the deck, unconscious.

Alexa, Gault, and Dave emerged from the pilothouse onto the deck. Dave's gun was pressed up against Alexa's head.

McDonald, Curt Terry and his crew glanced over and saw them, stunned looks on their faces.

Gault aimed his gun at McDonald. "Okay, we're back in the saddle," he said. "Toss your guns over the side."

No one moved.

Gault fired the Uzzi over their heads.

"The fuck you waiting for?" Gault said. "You want to see your daughter bleed, Weeb? 'Cause I'd be happy to make that happen."

Five automatic weapons were tossed over the side into the water.

Dave Gault backed toward the stern, his left arm tight around Alexa's neck, the knife still pressed up against her throat. Gault backpedaled between them and the crew, his Uzzi sweeping side to side. Dave and Alexa backed down the steps to the swimming platform. As Gault covered them, they climbed into Alexa's boat. Dave started up the engine.

Back in the pilothouse, one of Clay's eyes opened. Then the other. He struggled to get up. His head felt like a hangover after two bottles of rum. He staggered out of the pilothouse and ran to the safe house. He opened a closet, pulled out a sharp shooter's rifle with a scope and walked out.

Dave Gault thrust the accelerator forward on the Cigarette and the boat roared off, away from the ship.

Clay poked his head out at the highest point of the stern. He dropped to his knees, then flattened out and aimed the rifle. Through his scope, Clay looked for a shot at Dave, but Dave was still holding Alexa around the neck, her body shielding him.

Rafe was an easy shot, though. Clay thought about taking him out, but figured that Dave might then avenge it by killing Alexa.

Clay watched Gault, his eyes almost lustful, open one of the green duffel bags. Then he trained the rifle back on Dave. He could see Alexa looking right at him. He wondered if she could see him. He waited for Dave to release his grip on Alexa, when he thought he no longer needed a shield. But the boat was getting farther away, his shot more difficult by the second.

Then suddenly Alexa twisted out of Dave's grasp, and in a blink, kneed him in the groin, then dove to the deck.

Before she had even landed, Clay pulled the trigger. A single bullet ripped into Dave's forehead.

Clay turned the rifle on Gault, who was lunging toward Alexa.

Clay exhaled, his finger on the trigger. But before he could squeeze, a shot rang out from somewhere near him.

Gault staggered, dropped his gun, then fell over the side of the Cigarette. Clay turned to his right and saw his father, in a prone position twenty feet away, holding the other sharp shooter's rifle. McDonald was lying right next to him, looking through binoculars at his daughter.

"Nice goin', Pop. Where'd you learn to shoot like that?"

"Your memory's not so hot, I guess," Curt said. "Behind the house, you and me taking out Budweiser cans with 22's. Taught you everything you know."

Clay smiled and nodded. The three looked out and saw the Cigarette coming toward them, Alexa at the wheel. They ran down to the swimming platform as Alexa pulled up.

"You okay?" Clay asked. "That was a hell of a nutcracker, by the way."

"Thanks, that kickboxing came in handy," she said. "Now, can we just make sure Gault doesn't have any more relatives on board?"

Clay helped her off the boat. She was mussed up and shaken and Clay could tell her adrenaline was at a level he had never seen before.

McDonald wrapped his arms around his daughter. "Good goin', honey."

"Thanks, Daddy," she said.

As McDonald looked over her shoulder, he saw something dark and ominous rise up out of the water. "What the hell?"

Alexa, Clay, and Curt all swung around.

A jet-black submarine, looking like a sinister killer whale, rose up out of the water and surfaced on the port side. Clay grabbed Alexa's arm and the four of them ran up the steps. Curt shouted to one of the crew on the aft deck. "All hands to the stern! Armed and ready."

A few moments later Clay, Alexa, McDonald, Curt and the rest of the crew had taken positions at the stern. They were aiming an artillery of weapons at the submarine below. Clay had Gault's Stinger mounted on his shoulder.

Eleven dangerous-looking Hispanic men climbed out of the submarine, all aiming high-powered, automatic weapons back at the men on the *Miss Adventure*.

One of them—older, short, spiky hair—cupped his hands together and in a Spanish accent shouted, "I am looking for Rafe Gault?"

Clay glanced at his father, then McDonald. "You just missed him," Clay said.

The man, Ernesto Bacalou, looked confused.

"I dun understand. We s'posed a meet—"

"Gault is dead," Clay said. "You might run into him on your way out of here, floating down to the bottom."

"My men and me, we come on board. I want to see—"

"No, *senor*, nobody's coming on board," Clay said.

But Ernesto flicked his head for his men to follow him. Clay took a step forward, aiming the Stinger at Ernesto.

"In case you're wondering what this thing on my shoulder is, it's called a FIM 92A Stinger rocket launcher. It contains a twenty-two pound, directed-energy, blast fragmentation warhead," Clay said. "In plain English, that means it'll blow a hole in your little sub a fucking Hummer could drive through."

Ennesto hesitated, like he wasn't getting it.

Alexa stood up. "*Esa cosa fundira un agujero en su submarino que podria atravesar un...* fucking Hummer."

"So, *amigo*, it's time for you and your compadres to get the hell out of here," Clay said. "Get back in your little sub and go... *now*."

Clay glanced over at Alexa.

"*Es hora de salir a la carretera, amigo... lárgate de aquí ahora*."

Ernesto still didn't move.

Clay glanced over at Gault's Cigarette boat twenty feet away. He swung the Stinger at it and pulled the trigger.

There was a massive explosion and the boat was obliterated into hundreds of tiny pieces that rained down slowly into the ocean.

Ernesto's eyes bulged seeing the boat reduced to toothpicks. He flicked his head, then he and his men retreated to the sub's hatch and scurried down the ladder.

Alexa looked at Clay, then her father. "Excuse my language, Daddy," she said, "I was just translating."

THIRTY-FOUR

AT THE SWIMMING PLATFORM, Gault's head popped up out of the water. Gritting his teeth, he planted his hands on the platform and, slowly and painfully, hoisted himself out of the water. His shoulder was bleeding. He looked around and saw a balled up towel. He ripped it in half and wrapped a strip around his wounded shoulder. He reached down and pulled an automatic pistol out from an ankle holster.

Clay was behind the bar making drinks for McDonald, Curt, Harrow, and Alexa.

Gault staggered into the aft salon, holding his pistol unsteadily. He looked half dead, but on a mission, not to be denied.

He aimed his gun at Clay.

Clay, a bottle in hand, looked up and saw Gault.

The other four, their backs to Gault, saw the look in Clay's eyes.

They turned and saw Gault at the door of the salon.

Alexa gasped.

Gault took another step into the salon, his gun trained on Clay.

Clay, with the bottle still in one hand, glanced down below the level of the bar at his pistol lying there.

"What can I tell ya, man, old Rangers die hard," Gault said. "Sorry, hero, only one professional courtesy per lifetime."

He inched closer and aimed point-blank at Clay.

Charlie Harrow pressed the remote control card in his pocket.

The floor beneath Gault started to shift. Gault glanced down at it.

Clay, in a lightning move, grabbed his pistol and fired just once. He hit Gault square in the heart. Gault crashed backwards and went down hard.

This time, there was no doubt about it—Gault was dead before he hit the floor.

THIRTY-FIVE

TWO CREWMEN DRAGGED Gault's body away.

As Clay watched them, his cell phone rang. He looked down at it. "Anthony Nobbis" on the caller ID. He had one percent left.

"I was wondering what happened to you, Anthony."

"You have anything to do with waxing that ISIS guy, Clay? Bashir ben Nadal," Nobbis asked.

Clay thought for a second, then smiled. "No, but I'll give you a coupla other scoops. Twelve pirates took over this yacht I'm on—"

"What?"

"Yeah, then this senator had a fight with a Gila monster named Harold the Horrendous. After that this Mexican drug lord pulled up in a black sub—"

"Very funny, Clay," said Nobbis. "You can go back to the tequila now."

Clay hung up, shook his head and walked over to Alexa. She grabbed his arm and turned to her father.

"Okay, you're on your own now," she said. "Any more bad guys come on board, you handle 'em? Clay didn't fly forty hours to hang out with a bunch of gnarly old farts."

Clay laughed and put out his hand to McDonald.

"Pleasure shooting with you, Webb. You did all right for a quail guy." Then he turned to Charlie Harrow. "Senator, you got my vote any day," Clay shook Harrow's hand, then turned to his father. "And Pop, glad we patched things up. But you might wanna get those Budweiser cans out again, practice up a little on your shooting."

Curt laughed. "Wiseass."

Clay was at the wheel of Alexa's boat. He put his arm around her and pulled her close. "So I been thinking... maybe we have a little party."

"Oh, yeah?" said Alexa.

"No, a big party. Coupla tents, lots of bubbly. Bridesmaids in cute little pink dresses."

Alexa's mouth formed a big, wide smile. "There was everything but a proposal in there."

"Yeah, yeah, I'm workin' up to it. No one ever said I was the quickest guy around."

She rolled her eyes. "Ah, I'm pretty sure they have."

Clay laughed. "You know what—"

Alexa put her finger up to his lips.

He puts both arms around her, their lips met and... *Omigod, now that was a kiss.*

Off in the distance, the *Miss Adventure* was a smoking carcass and whole sections of it were destroyed.

Undeterred, though, a golfer teed up a ball and smacked it two hundred and fifty yards out into the azure blue water. Another man was leisurely swimming laps in the pool that had no diving board, and Jess stood on a deck with a shotgun to her shoulder.

"Pull," she said and blasted the clay pigeon into tiny, little pieces.

THE END

CHARLESTON NOIR SAMPLE CHAPTERS

(NICK JANZEK CHARLESTON MYSTERIES BOOK 3)

ONE

SHE WAS BREAKING her ironclad law: Never let a man step foot into her penthouse apartment on King Street. But, in this case, it didn't really matter, since her visitor wouldn't be leaving on his own steam.

Which was to say, vertically.

She remembered his cockiness from fourteen years before.

The way he sat on a horse—all loose and smirky and self-assured, like he was goddamn Roy Rogers or something. And the way he looked her over that first time, his stare stripping away her tank top and jean cut-offs. And those two other cretins with him…like he was the sheriff and they were the posse.

He was drunk now—really drunk—his washed-out blue eyes cruising the room after just having tried to paw her. She had shoved him away but knew he'd try again. He seemed to focus every once in a while, but, she could tell, he was mostly seeing blurs.

"What's that thing?" he asked, pointing to an expensive tortoise-shell box on her mantel.

"A tea caddy," she said, stifling a yawn.

"Doesn't look like any of the caddies up at Yeaman's," he said with a smirk.

It was a lame joke. Yeaman's Hall was a prestigious golf club north of Charleston where all the local blue bloods and rich Yankees played.

Fourteen years ago—when she was sixteen—he'd seemed like the coolest guy she'd ever run across. He didn't say much back then. He let that rich-kid swagger and arrogance do the talking, and she'd been impressed.

"What are those blue and white things?" He pointed to an expensive Delft Garniture set.

"Dutch porcelain figurines," she said.

"Look like pieces from an old chess set," he said.

She glanced over at them. *Yeah, if you're drunk, stupid, and totally unsophisticated, they do.*

She'd had enough of his blather as she watched him take another pull of his Maker's Mark. Now was as good a time as any.

She stood up and straightened her skirt, because she could see he was getting itchy to start pawing her again.

"Where you goin'?"

"To powder my nose," she said, not looking back.

He smiled, thinking that was code for getting prepped to do the deed.

She walked across the room, opened the mahogany door, and closed it behind her.

He looked around the room at a few framed pictures of her with people he didn't recognize. Then his eyes lit on one of her riding a horse. She looked to be in her teens. That was how old she'd been when they first met. He was surprised she didn't seem to have any bad feelings about what happened back then. Come to think of it...how could she *not?*

He looked at his watch and wondered what she was doing besides powdering her nose.

A moment later, the bathroom door opened and a man in blue jeans and a Lacoste shirt strode out.

He had a pool cue in one hand and something long, sharp, and shiny in the other.

TWO

NICK JANZEK WAS on his way to the Charleston police station on Lockwood at seven in the morning when he got the call from the dispatcher. She told him in short, choppy but detailed sentences that a woman who had been walking her dog in White Point Garden in the Battery had called in a possible homicide. The woman had been unusually specific, the dispatcher said. She'd first noticed the vic on a bench reading a book. Something about him made her keep an eye on him, she explained. A minute or two later, as she watched him out of the corner of her eye, he suddenly pitched forward, holding his book in a "vice grip," and his forehead "bounced" on the macadam pathway. The caller ran up to the body and saw a gash on the man's forehead but not one drop of blood.

Janzek, doing seventy down Murray Boulevard, pulled up to White Point Garden and skidded to a stop next to a black and white Charger. He saw a uniform talking to a woman with a dog and walked over to join them. The cop's name was Robert Prioleau.

As he got closer, he saw a man's body on the pavement behind the two.

"Hey, Robert," Janzek said, looking down at the body.

"Nick," Prioleau said, nodding. "This is Ms. Hobbes. She came in here to walk her dog about a half hour ago and found the deceased."

Janzek looked up from the body to the woman.

"Hello, Ms. Hobbes, I'm Detective Janzek," he said, pulling out his murder book and pen from his inside jacket pocket. "Can you tell me exactly what happened from the moment you first got here? Just one second, please—" he turned to Prioleau— "Tape off the scene, will you, Robert? Keep everyone out of here." Then he turned back to the woman. "I'm sorry, you came here to walk your dog and—"

"I saw this man sitting on the bench here and didn't think much of it," she said. "Then as I was walking past him I said, 'good morning' and he didn't look up or say anything back. So I kept going and walked past him again later and the man hadn't moved. I mean, literally not moved an inch. I got the feeling he hadn't turned a page in his book either. Something about him was strange, not just that he didn't look up or say anything."

"But his eyes were open?" Janzek asked.

"Yes."

"Just that he hadn't moved?"

"Yes, he was dead still," she said, then realizing what she had just said, nodded. "Dead is right."

"So then what happened, Ms. Hobbes?" Janzek asked.

"So then, my dog, Haimish, went up to the man and, you know, kind of sniffed him. I pulled the leash back and at the same time I did, the man fell forward," Hobbes said. "His head hit first, really hard. It ended up facing to the side and I saw this big cut, but there was no blood at all."

"So that's when you called us?"

"No, first, I went to see if I could help him," Hobbes said. "I thought maybe he had fallen asleep on the bench, though his eyes were still wide open. But at that point I could just tell...."

"That he was dead?"

"Yes, not breathing at all," she said. "And when I touched him, he was cold...and stiff."

"Like he had been dead for a while?"

She nodded.

"So then you called?"

She nodded again.

Janzek looked down at the dead man. His eyes were still open and Janzek saw dried blood spatter on his pants below the crotch. He heard the blare of sirens. One was coming from the north, the other from the east.

He put on a pair of latex gloves, squatted next to the man, and patted him for a wallet. Feeling a bulge in a back pocket of the man's pants, he reached into the pocket and pulled it out. He found a South Carolina license in the plastic window. It said James M. Swiggett and gave his address. He returned the wallet to the man's pants and looked up at Ms. Hobbes.

"When you first got here, before the man fell over, were there other people in the park?"

"No, I didn't see anyone until a few minutes after I got here. It was just starting to get light."

"And can you describe those people?"

Hobbes pushed a strand of hair out of her eyes.

"One was a woman jogger. In her twenties, I'd say. Running fast, didn't even slow down," Hobbes said. "Then an older woman pushing a baby carriage. Like maybe she was a nanny or something."

"And that was all?"

Hobbes nodded. "Until Officer Prioleau got here."

Janzek glanced around. The curious had started to gather. There were six people outside the yellow tape that Prioleau had strung.

"Well, thank you very much, Ms. Hobbes. Can you give me your phone number and an email address in case I have more questions, please?"

"Sure," Hobbes said. "What do you think could have happened to him?"

"At this stage, I really have no idea," Janzek said. "But I appreciate all your help."

She gave him her cell number and email and, as Janzek was taking them down he heard steps behind him and turned.

It was his partner, Delvin Rhett.

Rhett was a bespectacled, trim black man in his late twenties who sported a fu manchu; Janzek suspected it was to make up for his otherwise scholarly look. A cop had once called him Urkel, meaning the nerdy kid Steve Urkel from an old TV sitcom. Janzek figured the fu manchu and Rhett's occasional sprinkling of ghetto-speak into conversations were his partner's attempt at countering the Urkel charge. He wore khaki pants, a white button-down shirt, a tie that was not perfectly centered, and a loose-fitting brown corduroy jacket. Superfly, he was not.

"Hey, Delvin," Janzek said, nodding to him, "this is Ms. Hobbes, the witness who called it in."

Rhett nodded. "Hello, Ms. Hobbes," he said, then got down in a crouch next to the victim. His eyes went right to the spots of blood on the victim's pants.

Ms. Hobbes nodded and smiled at Delvin, then moved away with her dog and ducked under the yellow tape.

Rhett looked up at Janzek. "Strange place to see blood."

Janzek nodded, got down next to him, and pointed at the victim's forehead. "Yeah, but not a drop from that cut."

Rhett nodded. "Never seen a guy so pale before," he said. "Like Casper."

"Who?"

"The friendly ghost."

Rhett had an offbeat sense of humor and Janzek was still trying to warm up to it. They had been together a little over a year.

"Guy's name is James Swiggett. Looks like he bled out somehow before he took the header on the pavement."

"So someone brought him here, you figure?" Rhett asked. "Already dead?"

"That's my guess," Janzek said as Rhett pulled out his cell phone and started snapping pictures.

As he watched, Janzek noticed a goose-egg-size bump on the top of the man's head.

"Get a few of this, too," Janzek said to Rhett, pointing to the bump. "Looks like a tree fell on the poor bastard."

"Yeah, or a Louisville Slugger."

"I wanna show you something else." Janzek's old football knee popped as he stood. He took a few steps down the path, Rhett following, then pointed at a tire-track imprint next to the macadam path.

Rhett's eyes followed the tire track. "Goes right up to the bench."

"Yeah," Janzek said, crouching down to inspect it. "But the tires are too close together to be a car or a truck."

"And who would drive a car or a truck into the park anyway?" Rhett asked. "A uniform spots it and he's all over the guy."

"I'm guessing a golf cart," Janzek said.

Golf carts were a common means of transportation in downtown Charleston.

"Yup. That'd fit," said Rhett.

"I'm gonna go check the surrounding area," Janzek said, "see what else I come up with."

Rhett nodded and started taking snapshots of the tire tracks.

Janzek didn't find anything else related to the dead man in the park, but at the far end he came across a large monument he'd never noticed before. It commemorated the hanging, on this site, of twenty-two pirates back in 1718. Their captain was Stede Bonnet. One of the things Janzek liked about Charleston was that it had a lot of history, much of it infamous. The monument noted that there had been twenty-nine pirates, but only the twenty-two had been hanged. Janzek wondered what happened to the other seven.

He glanced over at the dead body a football field away. The tradition of violent death in the beautifully-landscaped park was still going strong.

THREE

BILLY HOBART HAD BEEN through the house on lower Meeting Street with the realtor twice before. This time they'd be meeting Miranda Bennett there.

The Miranda Bennett.

From one of the oldest families in Charleston.

Billy and the realtor were up on the second floor when Miranda walked in the open front door.

"Yoo-hoo, Billy, the checkbook has arrived." Miranda warbled in her signature, free-spirited voice.

Billy walked down the steps from the second floor, the realtor trailing along behind him.

"Hey, honey," Billy said, walking down the steps and wrapping Miranda in a big hug. "Get that checkbook out and start writing. There's gonna be lots of zeroes in this offer. I'm thinking a million four. They don't take it, well then, screw 'em."

He looked over at the realtor.

"Oh, Mark, this is my friend Miranda Bennett," Billy said.

"Hello, Mrs. Bennett, pleased to meet you," said Mark, the chinless realtor from a nondescript office in West Ashley, clearly impressed to meet the grand dame of Church Street. She had the nicest house "on the bricks," as opposed to the slightly less-desirable houses a little further north on the paved section of Church Street.

Miranda shot chinless Mark a curt nod, her standard acknowledgement for the sub-classes, which included real-estate agents, waiters, hairdressers, and people who worked for the Department of Motor Vehicles.

"What are we going to sell it for, once you've worked your magic?" she asked Billy.

Billy glanced at chinless Mark. "Two million five, maybe. I don't know, what do you think, Mark?" Billy asked, testing the agent. "Assuming new HVAC—" heating, ventilation and air conditioning—"a refurbished kitchen and baths, plus a fountain to make that backyard fabulous?"

The agent was licking his chops at the prospect of getting a two and a half million-dollar listing once Billy fixed it up and put it back on the market. "At least that much," he said.

Billy frowned and shook his head. "Nah, on second thought, best case is two million two." He turned back to Miranda and lowered his voice so the agent couldn't hear. "The good news is I figure we'll only need to put three hundred thousand into it."

Miranda—sixty, savvy, rich, and thirty pounds overweight—hooked her arm onto Billy's.

"You know I'm lousy with numbers, honey," she said, "so how much does that mean we make?"

"Net around four hundred thousand," he said. The reality was closer to six hundred thousand, but four hundred was certainly enough to get Miranda to stroke a nice, fat check.

Their deal was that Miranda would put up all the money and get a guaranteed fifteen percent return. That would mean that she'd get around ninety thousand and he'd get the rest—five hundred ten thousand. Not bad, particularly since he didn't have to put up a dime.

Miranda liked the money, but what was more important to her was the fact that she got the companionship and attention of a good-looking thirty-year-old man. Billy, at five ten, had a slight build, but was rakishly handsome—high cheekbones, brilliant blue eyes, and thick, wavy blond hair. Miranda still wasn't totally clear about his sexuality.

"So how much should I make the check out for?" Miranda asked Billy.

Billy looked at the realtor.

"How much do you think?" Billy asked chinless Mark. Another test.

"I don't know, I'd say twenty thousand would be a meaningful deposit," Mark said.

"I'd say *too* meaningful." Billy turned to Miranda, "Make it ten thousand, honey."

Mark started to say something but stopped.

"Who to?" Miranda asked.

"Carolina One Trust Account," Mark said.

Miranda signed the check with a flourish and looked up. "So, Billy, will you use Tipton for the sale on this?"

Billy nodded, and Mark looked as if he'd just been pick-pocketed. "Absolutely. Girl's the best realtor in town." He turned back to Mark. "Since we're all cash buyers and it's gonna be an easy deal for you, we're gonna need you to take a four percent commission."

Mark reacted like Billy had not only snatched his wallet, but grabbed all his loose change, too.

"Oh, I can't do that," Mark said, "my broker would never go along with it."

Billy started walking toward the door. "Come on, Miranda. I guess we'll have to go buy that one up on Tradd Street instead."

Mark moved swiftly to block the door. "Wait, wait," he said. "Let me see what I can do."

Tipton Hill had been the highest producer at Carriage Properties for the past three years. She was in her late twenties, unmarried and possessed of near model-like good looks. Few people wondered if this beauty helped her stellar sales record. She was showing the Bingham house to Donald Knott, who ran a big fund up in New York. It was

Knott's third time seeing the house and Tipton was eighty percent sure she'd be writing up an offer. They were in the Bingham house's living room, which featured fine English furniture and more books than Tipton had ever seen in any Charleston house.

She slid a Thomas Pynchon novel out from a bookshelf. Yep, just as she expected, it was stiff…starchy, almost. Clearly, no one had gotten past the jacket copy.

Then something caught her eye that she hadn't spotted before, up on a shelf above her head. It was a penwork box, probably from the late 1700s, in a unique pagoda shape. A classic, she could tell at first glance, and she wondered if the owner knew what he had. It elicited a visceral response in her—her heart rate ticking up, nerves in her fingers jangling—and she felt an ardent yearning for it, approaching lust almost. A few times in the past she'd actually started sweating while picturing certain exceptional pieces owned by others placed in a prominent spot in her living room.

"How long's it been on the market?" Knott asked, snapping Tipton out of her reverie.

He had asked her that same question the first time he saw the house. He was a self-important and humorless man with an off-kilter handlebar mustache.

"Four and a half months," she said, knowing he loved numbers. "No offers so far. It works out to six hundred, sixty-five dollars per square foot. Last sale was in 2014 for two million, one hundred thousand. They redid the kitchen and the master bath at a cost of around ninety thousand at that time."

Knott did his best not to look impressed. "And what do the comps say?"

She put her hand on the back of a chintz loveseat. "They range from about six hundred twenty dollars to six hundred sixty a square foot," she said, watching him blink a few times, processing.

"So this is on the high side of that range," he said, slipping a book out of a bookshelf. It was a Robert Caro biography of LBJ and looked brand new. Knott put his hand on his chin, doing a poor Thinker impression. "Let's make 'em an offer of two million, seventy-five thousand," he said. "That works out to six hundred a foot."

Six hundred ten, actually, thought Tipton. Instead of correcting Knott, she did the quick math on the commission of a two million, seventy-five thousand dollar sale. It came out a one hundred, sixty-five thousand—eighty percent of which she's get for herself.

That money would go a long way to buying the furniture in the new house she was building, and she'd do anything necessary to make sure the deal went through.

FOUR

JANZEK WAS HANGING up his phone when Delvin Rhett walked into his office with two pieces of paper in his hand.

"You hear?" Delvin asked before Janzek had time to bring up the phone call he'd just ended.

Janzek looked at him. "Hear what?"

"Poor bastard got Bobbited."

Janzek leaned back in his chair. "What the hell does that mean?"

"Jesus, man, you haven't read this?" Rhett held up three sheets of paper. "Check your email. Lorena Bobbit was that pookie who cut off her hubby's John Henry Johnson."

Most of Rhett's patter Janzek could decipher, but sometimes it took a while. "Jesus. That's what happened to Swiggett?"

Rhett nodded.

It made a sick kind of sense, given all the blood they'd seen on the vic's pants.

Janzek reached for the pages. "Let me see that."

"You got it in your email," Rhett said. "Guy was four quarts low, too."

Janzek turned to his computer and clicked on his email. The first message he saw was from the Medical Examiner.

Rhett sat as Janzek started reading. It was one of the more gruesome write-ups Janzek had ever read. It confirmed that the vic was James McClain Swiggett. Janzek could only hope for Swiggett's sake that he was unconscious when the killer surgically removed his manhood—or, in the parlance of Delvin Rhett, his John Henry Johnson.

Janzek skimmed through the rest of the report, which was chock-full of blood and gore. The killer had apparently bludgeoned Swiggett, the ME speculated, then slashed his femoral artery, leading—as Janzek had previously surmised—to Swiggett bleeding out. *Exsanguinated*, as the ME termed it. The big question, of course, was where had it all happened. Figure that out and it would be case closed.

When he finished with the report, Janzek looked up at Rhett, who was on his iPhone checking messages.

"Hey, I need some time to go over this whole thing again," Janzek said. "How 'bout you come back in fifteen minutes and we'll talk it over."

Rhett nodded. "Killer's one sick mofo," he said, getting up. "Aight, check you later."

Janzek read through the report carefully this time. Then he did some internet research. The first thing he learned was that if someone lost one-third to half of his blood, he was going to die. The obvious conclusion that Janzek came to was that this had been no spur-of-the-moment murder. Whoever killed Swiggett had a well-thought-out plan, a key part of which was to execute it in a place where no trace of blood would ever be found. A place where multiple quarts of blood would drain away. A bathtub was the first place that came to mind.

Janzek thought back to the infamous John Wayne Bobbitt incident. At the time, he had been working a particularly grisly murder/suicide up in Boston. Flash forward to a little over a year ago, when Janzek put Boston in the rearview mirror and signed on with the Charleston PD. A series of devastating incidents had taken place up there to make him want a change of scenery—the worst being the murder of his wife. Twenty-five years before that, his father, who had been a "close personal associate" of the murderous mobster, Whitey Bulger, had been killed execution-style in an alley behind a bar in

Waltham. Whitey himself was a leading suspect. But then he disappeared. There were just too many ghosts in Boston for Janzek so he packed up a U-Haul truck, hitched his car behind it, and headed south.

At six feet and a solid one hundred seventy-five pounds, Janzek had emerald-green eyes and dark hair he wore on the long side. A two-inch scar from below his eye ran down the left side of his face and stopped just above a sturdy cleft chin that had taken a few shots over his forty years of hard living.

His mind wandered back to Bobbit again. Aside from all the jokes on Letterman and Leno, he recalled thinking that Bobbitt must have been incredibly abusive and aggressively unfaithful to warrant that kind of punishment.

He didn't hear Rhett walk in.

"Pretty fuckin' sick, huh?"

Janzek looked up, startled. "Jesus, man," he said, "they got this thing called knocking."

"Sorry. Readin' all that shit freaked you out, huh?" Rhett smiled. "What's the matter, you never had a dickless vic before?"

"Okay, Delvin, can it, will you? Let's talk about what we got and what we're gonna do next."

While the M.E. and techs had been preparing their gruesome report, Delvin and Janzek had dug up plenty on the vic over the last twenty-four hours.

James McClain Swiggett, thirty-four, was a lawyer who specialized in tax law. He had gone to Porter-Gaud, the private school in nearby West Ashley, then to the University of Virginia, and after that, UVA's law school. He seemed like a typical rich kid and, from what Janzek was able to piece together, had conducted a pretty serious party-hearty lifestyle, along with a few run-ins with the law. He'd had a DUI seven years back and had been the defendant in a paternity suit four years before that. All this while married and bringing up three sons.

In the breast pocket of the Swiggett's blue blazer, a crime-scene tech found a couple of tabs of something called Rohypnol and another called Nymphomax, whose ingredients, Janzek learned, were designed to get women in the mood. *Bill Cosby specials*, Rhett called them.

Janzek's initial working theory was that Swiggett had a date with someone he was not married to and planned to ply her with more than just a few cocktails. Rhett theorized that maybe in the middle of Swiggett's tryst, a husband or a boyfriend had caught the pair in the act, then spared the woman and killed Swiggett. Only problem with that theory was it was spur-of-the-moment and he felt that Swiggett's murder was premeditated.

Elaborately premeditated, in fact.

"You're lost in thought. Whatcha thinking?"

Janzket nodded at his desk phone. "I just got a call from a bartender at the Carolina Yacht Club on East Bay. He read about the murder and told me Swiggett had a drink there with some other guy at around seven the night of."

"Did he know who the other guy was?"

"No, he didn't," Janzek said. " I asked him to describe him and he wasn't much help. Blond guy, around thirty, on the short side. Then I asked him who else was in the bar at the same time. Thinking maybe someone else could ID him."

"Any luck?"

"Yeah, he gave me a list of five people there. I'm gonna start calling them, then go pay a visit to Swiggett's widow. Meanwhile, why don't we split up the people in Swiggett's law firm?" Janzek handed Rhett a printout of the partners and associates he had found listed on the office's website. "I'll take A through M, you take the rest."

Rhett nodded as he read through the list.

Janzek looked out his window and saw a new hotel being built in the distance. Charleston had been booming in the year he had been there while the rest of the country seemed to be limping along.

Janzek swung back to Rhett. "I also got a list of names and numbers of all residents within a half mile of the park," Janzek said. "That's about three hundred phone calls. We can split those up, too. You take two hundred, I'll take a hundred."

Rhett groaned. "Oh, gee, Nick. Thanks. That's real fair."

"Hey, you're a much better talker than me."

Rhett shook his head in weak protest.

Janzek shrugged. "Nobody ever said this was a glamorous gig, my friend."

FIVE

AFTER MAKING five unsuccessful calls to bar-goers who might have seen Swiggett's blond drink-mate on the night of his murder, Janzek paid a visit to the vics widow on James Island. Camille Swiggett lived in a modest two-story brick house in Riverland Terrace, one of the more desirable areas of the Charleston suburb.

Janzek was surprised at the plainness of Swiggett's house based on two things: One, how the dead man had been dressed when discovered in White Point Garden. He'd been wearing a Brooks Brothers blue blazer, a yellow Hermes tie, and expensive-looking English shoes. Two, the fact that he was a lawyer. But then Janzek remembered something that his boss, Chief of Police Ernie Brindle, had told him when he first got to Charleston. Something about how lawyers, for the most part, were a dime a dozen in Charleston, and the only ones who made real money were the ambulance chasers. The others just got by.

Swiggett's house was nice enough but certainly not fancy, and it had a wooden accessibility ramp leading up to a side entrance. Camille Swiggett opened the front door and let him in wordlessly. Janzek caught a glimpse of an old man hooked up to a respirator through a half-opened door off of the living room. Camille was blonde, pretty, slightly overweight, with dead eyes, slumped shoulders, and a whispery, forlorn voice. Her beaten-down first-impression formed a surprising mismatch with how forthcoming she was about her husband. It almost seemed as if she wanted to be the one to put her husband's secrets out there and on the record before someone else dug them up. Without mincing words, she began by telling Janzek that her husband was a serial philanderer. Within the first three minutes of their conversation, she told him that she had found out Swiggett had cheated on her the night before their wedding fourteen years before.

He wished all his interviewees were so forthcoming.

Camille speculated that her husband's proclivity to stray far and wide had something to do with his death. Janzek even thought he heard a note of 'he got what he deserved' in her tone. He asked her about the events of the night Swiggett was killed. She said they'd had an early dinner at six o'clock in front of the TV, then Swiggett had taken a shower and said he was going to go meet a friend for a drink at the Yacht Club on East Bay Street. She'd suspected the friend might be a woman, but she hadn't bothered questioning him further.

Janzek asked her if she had any idea who the woman might have been. She had four candidates and allowed that there were likely others she didn't know about. He wrote all the names down, figuring he and Rhett would split them up and interview them.

Following her candid admissions, he proceeded to ask all the standard questions: Did Swiggett have any enemies who might want to do harm to him? She answered that with a question: Two of the women he'd been sleeping with had husbands, so wouldn't they be possible suspects? She didn't know either of the women, but again volunteered that you never knew what a cuckolded husband might do…right? Unless, of course, the cuckold were *her* husband. Jamie wouldn't have given a damn who Camille slept with. To which she added, "Well, late husband, I guess that would be."

He asked if there had been any incidents in the past, any threats on her husband's life, anything that she might have overheard or that he had told her about. She thought for a second, then answered no, not that she could think of.

He got brazen and asked if they'd had any money problems. Glancing around the house, he'd noticed how everything looked a little threadbare. Like maybe too much of their money went toward Jamie's wardrobe instead of a new carpet or replacements for the see-through curtains. Before Camille could answer he asked if Swiggett owed anyone money. Did he have any debts of any consequence?

That opened up the floodgates. Camille broke into a long, stream-of-consciousness ramble, starting with how she could barely afford to shop at Whole Foods any more. How between taking care of her father-in-law, who had no insurance but huge medical bills, and Jamie insisting that their kids, Brett and Olivia, go to the expensive private schools—Porter-Gaud and Ashley Hall, respectively—they'd come perilously close to a hand-to-mouth existence.

What had gone so wrong? she bemoaned. After all, Jamie had grown up rich. His parents had had three houses. On Sullivan's Island, across the bridge from Charleston, Boca Grande, Florida, not to mention the big hunting place down south. But then it all fell apart. She said how Jamie kept telling her not to worry, no need to put the kids in public schools, he was going to take care of everything. But she *did* worry. A lot, and, fact was, their financial situation had kept getting worse.

Just last week, he had stumbled home at eleven p.m.—"from one of his sordid little affairs," Camille said—and told her that this time he really meant it. *This* time, their financial problems were going to be over. He had never gotten around to telling her how this little miracle was going to happen. For her part, Camille had responded sarcastically: "Good, so does this mean I can buy dog food now?"

That was the first and only time Camille resorted to humor in the hour and fifteen minutes Janzek spent at her house...but maybe she hadn't been joking at all.

SIX

BILLY HOBART DIALED Miranda Bennett as he paced around his apartment on King Street, looking down at the boats on the Ashley River. Billy's contractor was about two months from finishing another house he was flipping on Atlantic Street and Billy, who had a nose for promoting his renovated houses, had just had a brainstorm.

Miranda's voicemail finally picked up and he left a message. As he waited for Miranda to call back, he went to the window that looked out over the tops of the live oak trees of White Point Garden. On the other side of the garden were three spectacular houses on South Battery that loomed up above the trees. They had to be five or six stories tall. Beyond them, he saw an enormous white structure. Incredibly, it was *moving*. That's when he realized it was a colossal Carnival cruise ship slowly steaming into its slip at 32 Washington Street. It would soon be disgorging the great unwashed—gawkers and selfie-snappers from New Jersey, Pennsylvania or wherever it was they came from—and dumping them onto the pristine, hallowed streets of Charleston. Later that day, the ship would raise its twenty-ton anchor and depart, its passengers nattily outfitted in their newly purchased, *Someone in Carolina Loves Me* T-shirts and sated on Market Street hot dogs and ice cream cones.

That *someone* in Carolina who loved them sure as hell was not Billy Hobart.

Miranda called him right back and said that she had been on the phone with "that stultifying bore, Weedie Cheslow."

Billy, still watching the monster ship dock, told her about his brainstorm. "Wouldn't it be fantastic if we had a big party at the house on Atlantic—like a giant open house—so people could come and see how fabulous it turned out? Maybe even sell it to someone who attends? Just think…we wouldn't even have to pay a broker's commission."

"But what about Tipton?" Miranda asked.

"Don't worry about Tipton," Billy said, "we give her plenty of business."

Miranda said she thought it was a marvelous idea and wondered why they hadn't done it before. Then she volunteered the use of her impressive Rolodex of who's-who in Charleston, which was, of course, Billy's whole point in suggesting the idea in the first place.

Suddenly, though, as if a light bulb had popped on over his head, he had an even better idea.

"Wait a minute…what if, instead of a big, fancy open house with all the movers and shakers of Charleston—along with the rich, nouveau Yankees who desperately want in on Charleston society—we make it a big, fancy benefit? It could be for the Preservation Society or...what's that illustrious do-gooder environmental group called?"

"Oh," Miranda said, "you mean the Conservation Coastal League?"

"Yeah, yeah, exactly, that's it," Billy said, his mind racing now. "What we could do is have a bunch of silent auction items that people or companies donate. Lay them out on big tables. You know, with a little piece of paper in front of the item where people write their bids. Then someone else comes along and writes down a higher bid below it? Well, you of all people know the drill."

"Of course, I do," said Miranda. "I've been to a million of 'em."

"The trick," he said, "is to get really good stuff."

"Yes, exactly," Miranda agreed. "I've been to ones where the silent auction stuff is all garbage. So we could go to a place like *Goat. Sheep. Cow.* and get them to donate a case of really good French wine."

"Absolutely," he said. "And get a nice, little tax donation and a bunch of free press."

"Or get somebody to donate a trip to somewhere really exotic and fabulous," Miranda said, really getting into it now. "Like St. Barth's or Anguilla or Harbor Island."

"Exactly," Billy said, though he didn't have a clue where the last two were. "Maybe a round of golf up at Yeaman's. Throw in a couple of lessons with the golf pro."

"I don't know," Miranda said. "That doesn't have much *panache* to it. We need to have the absolute best of everything. *Ne plus ultra*," she added enthusiastically.

"Definitely," agreed Billy, not sure what the phrase meant, but pretty sure it was French. He was still watching the Brobdingnagian cruise ship, which had come to a dead stop now, towering over the mighty houses south of Broad.

"Oh, it's *such* a marvelous idea, Billy, why in the world didn't we think of it before?" asked Miranda. "Throw a party, raise money for a good cause, and get a little publicity for our house. Win-win, for everybody."

"And you know what the key is, right?" Billy asked.

"What?"

"Booze," he said. "Lots and lots of top-shelf booze. That's what makes silent auctions so successful. Give 'em a few stiff ones, shed their inhibitions, makes everyone a little more competitive."

Miranda laughed. "Starting with a waiter serving flutes of champagne at the front door."

"Brilliant," he agreed, and then sprung the coup de grace on her. "What about having 101 Atlantic as the sole item in the *live* auction?"

Miranda went silent for a second, then said, "Oh my God, Billy. *You really are a genius*!"

A live auction typically featured an auctioneer, preferably clad in a dinner jacket, whose sole function was to incite spirited, inebriated bidders to grossly overpay for top-of-the-line items. Sometimes auctioneers were local celebrities, like a newscaster from the local TV station who could talk fast and rev up a crowd. But Billy and Miranda agreed that they would aim higher. Much higher.

"All right, then. I'll get to work on the silent-auction donors tomorrow," Billy said.

"Divine," Miranda said. "Oh, this is going to be *such* fun."

CHARLIE CRAWFORD - NEW YORK HOMICIDE

Download your free copy of Charlie Crawford - New York Homicide a Charlie Crawford prequel novella.

AFTERWORD

I hope you enjoyed Dead in the Water. If you wouldn't mind, I'd love a quick review on Amazon.

Next, I return to Charleston for the third in the Nick Janzek series. Nick and Delvin seem to be getting nowhere on the murder of a philandering lawyer. But it only gets worse with two more brutal homicides.

After that, we head back down to Palm Beach for Charlie Crawford's latest - a grisly murder inside a clandestine cult.

ABOUT TOM TURNER

A native New Englander, Tom dropped out of college and ran a bar in Vermont…into the ground. Limping back to get his sheepskin, he then landed in New York where he spent time as an award-winning copywriter at several Manhattan advertising agencies. After years of post-Mad Men life, he made a radical change and got a job in commercial real estate. A few years later he ended up in Palm Beach, buying, renovating and selling houses while getting material for his novels. While at a wedding, he fell for the charm of Charleston, South Carolina. He spent six years there and just completed his fourth book in the Nick Janzek series set in Charleston. Most recently, Tom headed down the road to Savannah, where he just finished a novel about lust and murder among his neighbors.

Learn more about Tom's books at:
www.tomturnerbooks.com

ALSO BY TOM TURNER

CHARLIE CRAWFORD PALM BEACH MYSTERIES

Palm Beach Nasty

Palm Beach Poison

Palm Beach Deadly

Palm Beach Bones

Palm Beach Pretenders

Palm Beach Predator

Palm Beach Broke

Palm Beach Bedlam

Palm Beach Blues

The Charlie Crawford Palm Beach Mystery Series: Books 1, 2 & 3

NICK JANZEK CHARLESTON MYSTERIES

Killing Time in Charleston

Charleston Buzz Kill

THE SAVANNAH SERIES

The Savannah Madam

STANDALONES

Broken House

Box Sets

For a current list of all available titles, please visit **tomturnerbooks.com/books**.

Made in the USA
Monee, IL
10 December 2020

51949643R00100